WITCH-FINDER

Vanessa Knipe

A Chronicle of the Staff and Students of
The Theological College
of
St. Van Helsing

BooksForABuck.com

2008

Vanessa Knipe

WITCH-FINDER

Vanessa Knipe

A Chronicle of the Staff and Students of
The Theological College of
St. Van Helsing

BooksForABuck.com

January 2009

ISBN: 978-1-60215-090-4

Contents

Granny's Secret for Perfect Vegetables

Rivalry was fierce amongst the villagers over this wretched vegetable competition, but sabotage was going too far. Pam peered at the man sprinting between the overgrown hedges. The only place the back lane led was her cousin's vegetable patch.

Leaning on the chipped porcelain sink, she craned her neck to see.

Halted by the gate, the man checked over his shoulder.

She tried to duck behind the summer dust smearing her cousin's kitchen window, but the movement must have caught his eyes. He looked straight at her. With a sharp glance back up the lane, he brushed his fingers over his lips then made a throwing gesture at her. Another look around, then he vaulted the gate. Two huge dogs hurdled it after him.

Pam's knuckles whitened around the handle of the sharp knife that she had been rinsing. Without thinking, she turned. The back door opened in her face. Cousin James strode into the kitchen, letting in what must have been the only breeze in the county; it sent the tea towels into a frantic dance. He gawked at the knife in her hand.

'No, Pamela I don't need that. Thanks, but I've already chosen my exhibits.' He displayed some tomatoes picked vine-and-all. 'Don't these look like prize winners?'

Pam slid the knife into the sink, feeling silly. What had she planned to do with it? James plucked a tomato and offered it to Pam. She popped it into her mouth then decided to ask him about the stranger. What came out was,

'They're good. How do you get them to grow so well?'

Pam blinked. What had made her say that? The fruit had a bitter aftertaste.

'I used our Granny's special fertilizer. Didn't your mother tell you about it?'

'Mother's not interested in growing things,' Pam said. 'She hires a gardener.'

'You need to come and look at my greenhouse after the show.' James checked his watch and dashed into the pantry. 'Where's that bloody basket? I'm going to be late for the judging. I left it to the last minute to pick my tomatoes, so they'd be fresh.'

'I'm going to walk down,' she said.

Grunts followed her by way of reply.

She was going to find that man. Perhaps she could recognize him at the village fête. She trotted down the garden and into the back lane, taking the short cut to fête over steps, built into the dry-stone wall, leading to the churchyard. Once there, the gravel path crunched beneath Pam's trainers. After the oppressive heat of the lane, the shade under the yew trees chilled her.

A growl sounded, low like distant thunder, from behind the nearest gravestone. A large hound sat on a neatly trimmed grave, sending shivers from Pam's ancestral memory of wolves.

Was it one of the saboteur's dogs?

4

It barred her path back to her cousin James's cottage. The growl started again as it stared at her. Pam stepped back, away from the beast, a step towards the solid safety of the church then another, keeping her eyes firmly on the dog. It stood and shook, rattling its chain collar. As Pam took another step back it paced forward, herding her.

A rustle sounded from among the yew trees and the saboteur stepped out.

'Shhh.' His hand touched the head of the dog and it silenced. Behind him, prowled another wolfhound. Both dogs looked to him for further instruction.

She turned on the glare, the one she used for importunate clients at the lawyer's office.

Unfazed, he studied her as his dogs had. A beard shadowed his chin and his blue jeans were baggy at the knees with worn hems, but he looked too clean to be a tramp.

From beyond the church, Pam heard the happy sounds of the village fête. Could she make it there before this man got her?

More footsteps ground into the gravel path. Both dogs growled again.

She braced for flight while they looked back along the path.

'Pamela!' Her cousin, James cradled his tomatoes in his arms—the basket must still be lost. 'What did you run off like that for?'

Seeing the dogs, he halted. It was nearly comical the way he tried to back away.

'James,' Pam said, intending to tell him about this man running down the back lane from his vegetable plot. She wanted to scream out, but her warning came out as a coughing fit. The stranger's hazel eyes glinted as they shifted away, as if he was shy, but Pam saw he was laughing at her.

'You needn't worry about the boys,' he said, a gravelly Scots burr in his voice. 'They're softies really.'

The iron gate to the Vicarage garden squeaked on its hinges behind her.

'Dunkley, there you are.'

The stranger looked up and nodded politely. Pam twisted round, relieved to see the Vicar. He pushed back a strand of his gray hair, which had fallen over his eyes, as he took in the small gathering.

'Mr. Dunkley has agreed to help me judge our vegetables today, as the profits of our fête will be donated to the church roof fund. He's the foremost expert on gargoyles in the country.' The Vicar waved at the badly weathered gargoyles that jutted from the time-battered roof of his church.

The Vicar noticed James trying to slip away. 'That's right, you should be down there already. Everyone else is set up.

James edged past the dogs, white-eyed.

'That's the last of our competitors rounded up. Shall we go, Dunkley?' asked the Vicar.

Accompanied by the Vicar, Dunkley strolled across the grass with the grace of a lion inspecting the herds. The wolfhounds gave Pam a last filthy look and trotted after him. Watching as he left, she saw his hair was drawn back into a snaky plait that fell to his waist.

Pam frowned and ran a fingertip over a gravestone so worn the inscription could no longer be made out. What had stopped her from telling James about the stranger who had turned out to be a fête judge? Still puzzling, she followed the men.

Today, the Vicarage garden was thrown open, displaying borders overgrown with buddleia and fuchsia. On the neatly mown grass someone had laid shabby mattresses under a greasy pole set up between two trestles. There, the second of James's six kids was clobbering another child with a pillow.

Pam found Marjory, her cousin's wife, in the refreshment tent, cuddling the youngest of the brood, barely two. She looked too pale in this heat.

And no wonder, thought Pam, up and about so soon after her hysterectomy.

'I've done the dishes,' Pam said sitting with Marjory. 'You don't look well. I'm not an expert but maybe you should go back to bed.'

'What and leave you and *my* husband to get together?' she hissed. 'The pair of you with your Granny's magic recipe for growing tomatoes! I tried for years to obey his nonsense, and he repays me by turning away the moment I can't have any more children. Isn't six enough for him? Well, I'm not going to make it easy for you.'

Pam's mouth dropped open. The female volunteers turned to stare at them instead of serving the endless cups of tea and homemade sandwiches and cakes needed to lubricate the smooth running of the village fête. Marjory pushed back her chair and stood, still glaring at her husband's cousin.

'I'm going to find my children. It's time you thought about your own children, you home wrecker.' Tears streamed down Marjory's face as she stormed off.

'But...' *I don't know what you mean*, Pam didn't get to say.

Suddenly, no one was looking her way, everyone was discussing the gathering clouds. Would the rain hold off for the rest of the fête, was the question on everyone's lips.

Pam fled.

A few half-hearted drops of rain marked the tent canvas. Ducking under the entrance canopy to the Produce Marquee, she fanned her face—if only the cloud cover meant the heat would ease.

Through the canvas walls she heard, 'Are you sure?' That sounded like the Vicar.

'I tasted it in his tomatoes.' There was no mistaking Dunkley with his Scots accent.

'I was right, then.' The Vicar sighed.

'It's close to release, but that's my problem,' said Dunkley. 'That's why you called the office with your suspicions. He's not the only one.'

'These country parishes still do things the old way. When I called the office, I had no idea to expect you, sir.'

'Sometimes it's nice to be assigned a simple case.'

Pam was still frowning as they left the tent. The competitors filed in to see the results, James among them, looking smug. Two minutes later, he emerged shredding his entry form. Looking around, he saw Pam and demanded,

'Where's Marjory? I warned her.'

'Looking for your kids. Why don't you help her for a change?' Pam snapped.

He glared at her for a moment, then stalked off.

Pam stared after him.

He brushed past Dunkley who was walking back towards the Produce Marquee.

Dunkley glanced between James and another glum competitor who had followed James from the tent.

Dunkley made his choice—he caught the other man. 'I would like to discuss the various ways of cheating.'

The man grimaced. 'I didn't mean to cheat. I was just sick of James winning all the time. I spied on him in his shed…'

Pam wanted, no, *needed* to know what was going on here. The answer had to be in James's garden. She ran to the iron gate and back into the churchyard.

A breeze finally brought relief from the stifling heat, but wafted the stench of decaying leaves to her wrinkling nose.

She jumped as the lowest branches of the yew trees, which over hung the path, stroked her hair. The breeze carried a giggle up from the village fête— after all a breeze could not giggle itself. The sound, and the breeze blew away, leaving Pam alone with the hazy clouds darkening into thunder. Without that breeze there was no relief from air too heavy to breathe.

She strode along the back lane, determined to discover the source of the madness.

James's vegetable patch was away from the house. The main garden had bare grass, with a swing and a slide for the children. An orchard of five trees shielded the straight lines of produce from ball games.

It was set out as a potager, in square beds with grass paths between them. Strings with fluttering foil bird scares were stretched across winter vegetable seedlings. His shed and greenhouse stood in the center squares of the plot and a compost heap was set against the back fence.

From the relative poverty of the household furnishings, she had expected his outhouses to be cobbled together from old scrap, but this garden was where the money was spent. The prized, but not prize-winning, tomato plants grew like soldiers under pristine glass.

Wind scuttled through the bird scares. For a moment, it blew from snow-topped mountains. Then the stifling heat returned, as if the clouds were the lid on a box with no air holes.

Pam looked around for something strange, anything to explain the craziness and saw a rain front chasing her.

She ducked inside the shed as rain spotted her thin, cotton shirt.

The inside was as neatly kept as the garden outside, except for the strange pictograms, like Egyptian writing, chalked on the interior wall.

A circle had been gouged into the dirt floor. The focus of the drawings was a shelf in the back corner, where James had stood a statue of an old woman.

Pam stared at the statue, trying to remember if there was a patron saint of gardening.

The shed door slammed, clattering the tools that hung on nails. Pam glanced back, expecting that the mischievous breeze had blown it closed, but James stood there, blocking the exit.

'My spirit told me you had come up here.' He eyed her tight-fitting jeans.

That breeze that followed James everywhere was now trapped in the shed with them; despite well-fitting windows, it was drafty.

The breeze whispered, 'Here. Now.'

'Yes,' he said. 'We'll do the ritual here.'

From the way he guarded the door she expected him to make a pass but didn't mean to give him a chance.

'What ritual?' She tried to elbow him aside. 'Get out of the way.'

'You'll get wet.' He barred her retreat. 'Our Granny was a witch, you know.'

'Don't be silly.'

'Her familiar spirit needs a fertility ritual.' He spoke as if she had said nothing. 'To keep my garden in prime condition, it demands a placenta on the compost heap.'

Right, she thought, desperately checking to see if the windows opened. They were screwed shut. Step one: humor mad cousin. Step two: move him aside.

She forced a smile. 'I thought a fertility ritual would require a virgin.'

The mad breeze urged, 'Kiss her, kiss him.'

'Virgins! What nonsense! It needs a proven mother, like you.'

'I have a partner.' Her voice sounded squeaky. 'I'm happy with him. I don't do unfaithful.'

'I wouldn't need to do this if Marjory could have more children.' He grabbed for her.

'You're mad,' Pam screamed and tried to side-step him. Her hip banged into the potting table, slowing her.

James caught her in a bear hug, plastering his lips to hers.

She turned her face away so he got her ear, her cheek, but not her lips, but that didn't help much. His kisses burned her face like poison.

Pressing her against the table, James got his free hand onto the zip of her jeans. Her fist hammered against his shoulder; her other hand groped for a weapon as he pushed the waistband of her trousers over her hips.

A trowel touched her fingertips. Clutching it, she stabbed her cousin's arm.

He released her with a howl, his eyes promising repayment for the pain.

She yanked a spade from the wall.

Seeing her intention, he raised an arm to ward off the head blow. The force still slammed him to the floor.

Dropping the spade, she scrambled for the door. All the while the breeze whistled around her ears, making her head swim. She was sure it tried to hold her in the shed.

'No go,' sang the breeze.

One foot, then the next, she forced her way through the door.

The breeze strengthened but she made it.

Her jeans half-down, she flopped onto the grass path between vegetable beds. She thought of her partner and children, her house, the cold rain soaking through her thin summer clothes, anything to cover this singing in her ears.

Wind can't tell me what to do, Pam thought.

Reaching out, she clutched the nearest object, a clod of freshly dug earth. She flung it at the wind. Most of the mud flew through the wailing wind-thing, but some struck it. The wind became more solid, forcing it to take a hag shape.

What? Oh yes, air and earth were opposing elements.

She grabbed another clod and lobbed it at the air. More earth stuck to the creature. She scooped together a double handful and chucked it. The wind creature desperately fought against sinking towards the ground.

Applause sounded from the fence.

Dunkley was leaning on the barrier. 'I tried to get rid of it earlier, that's when you saw me. But he keeps it with him.'

Pam scrambled to her feet, hitching up her trousers as he opened the gate and strolled in, followed by his snuffling dogs.

They nosed at the ground and gruffed at the compost heap.

Thunk! James flung back his shed door and staggered into the garden. Blood from the spade-wound dripped down his ear into his cupped hands.

The sagging wind creature drifted to James. 'Master, give me blood for strength. I'm so weak.'

Noticing Dunkley, James screamed, 'Stay away from here!'

The wolfhounds growled, they paced over and sat between Dunkley and James.

James backed away from their white teeth.

'I'll do my job, then leave,' Dunkley said.

Pam stared as Dunkley advanced on the wind creature.

'Master, he'll kill me,' whispered the breeze. 'Blood, please master.'

James lifted his hand to the creature.

'No!' shouted Dunkley. 'You idiot!'

The creature lapped eagerly at James's hand. Clumps of earth fell away and it became translucent again.

'Now get him,' said James, pointing at Dunkley.

'FREE!' it sang. 'I'll free them all.'

The creature lifted its arms to the sky and began to spin. The thunderclouds that hung over the village reached down to embrace the twisting creature. Lightning crackled out from the point of contact. The wind tugged at Pam's hair, sucking the air from every breath.

She watched as a tornado was born.

It bore down on Dunkley.

He dived out of its way, grabbing Pam and pulling her to the ground. Grass tickled her cheek.

'It's going for the church,' shouted Dunkley, rolling to his feet.

James stared, open-mouthed at the funnel storm continued on the same route. Over the wind-roar he shouted, 'I said, *get him*.'

The windstorm stayed on course. It sounded like the rumble of bricks and mortar of a building being demolished—but the noise didn't end.

Over the roar, Pam heard screams from the direction of the church—people must have seen the monster bearing down on them.

'What about everyone at the village fête?' Pam reached up and grabbed Dunkley's arm. 'Do something! They'll all die!'

'It'll be worse than that if it wakes its kindred elementals.' Dunkley turned. 'Were you to be the sacrifice?'

'What?' Pam pursed her lips. 'He was going to do a fertility ritual, not kill me.'

With a glance at the stunned James, he pulled Pam to her feet. 'Stand there!'

Pam did as she was told, staring in horror as the twisting storm picked up speed. Dunkley darted to James, who backed away, but not quickly enough. Dunkley rubbed his hand down James's head covering his palm with James's blood.

In front of Pam, Dunkley studied the storm then checked his watch. '*Tuathal*.'

'Pardon?'

Dunkley looked at her. 'The storm is turning widdershins.' At her blank look he added, 'Anti-clockwise to you.'

He knelt in the mud and rubbed his hand on the ground clockwise, creating a small circle.

In the lane, the hedge lashed over grown branches. The storm tore out hawthorn stems, adding them to its destructive force.

Dunkley reached into a pocket with his clean hand and produced a whistle. He blew on it.

Pam's hair stood on end. At first she thought it was the clamor of the storm that blocked the sound, but the two wolfhounds lifted their heads and then trotted over to flank Dunkley. Then she understood, he was calling the storm to heel as if it were a recalcitrant dog.

The head of the storm still yearned to the church, but the base slid along the ground towards them. Overhead, lightning protested the windstorm's leashing.

Pellets of rain stung her cheeks and forehead.

Dunkley held his hand palm down, over the circle he had traced on the ground.

Pam cowered behind Dunkley.

He stood, a rock unbroken by the storm. Hawthorn branches gathered by the storm whipped out at him like thorny flails. He ducked one and sidestepped the next.

Above the circle he had drawn on the ground, he traced another circle, always moving his hand clockwise.

The storm thrashed about, ripping up the carefully laid out vegetable plots. The clouds reaching down to the creature began to untwist following the pattern of Dunkley's hand. The sky sucked them back up, abandoning the wind creature.

Over the fading roar of the storm, Pam heard James's wail.

Dunkley turned his hand over. The softening rain rinsed the blood away, then dripped into the circle drawing the hag down.

Pam heard scuffling behind her.

'No!' James screamed. He ran towards Dunkley.

Dunkley turned, automatically crouching, his eyes cold and watchful.

Without thinking, Pam bent and tugged on the bird scare string, tangling James's legs.

He sprawled among scattered cabbage seedlings.

The two wolfhounds came on guard and James stared straight into their snarls.

'Thank you.' Dunkley said, looking down at James.

'I didn't want you to hurt my cousin,' said Pam.

'I wouldn't have killed him.' Self-consciously, he rubbed his now-clean hand down his jeans. 'Now let's deal with this demon.'

'It's not a demon,' protested James as he struggled to disentangle himself from the string. 'It's a nature spirit. That's no reason to call in the demon hunters.'

'It is a demon, one that has been fed on the pain, fear and isolation of childbirth. I could taste its bitterness in your tomatoes. Another contestant used a *nature spirit*, one fed on honey. We chatted about cheating.' Dunkley looked at Pam. 'Finish it. Touch the air creature to ground.'

Warily, Pam slapped at the nearly solid hag. A flash, brighter than the sun, flared as the two opposites met. She winced away.

When it faded, a freshly carved gargoyle lay at her feet. Dunkley hefted it, then tucked it under one arm. Calling to his dogs, he walked to the garden gate.

Pam stared at him, open-mouthed. 'What are you?'

Dunkley looked over his shoulder, a hand on the gate latch. 'I'm...'

'He's a witch finder,' screamed James.

'Witch finder?' Pam's voice wavered. She looked at Dunkley.

His smile was wry but he didn't deny the charge.

'I work for the Church, certainly.'

'You're having me on. You hypnotized me, right? That's why I couldn't say anything.'

'Hypnosis, hmmm? You know, that's a fairly reasonable explanation.'

'Is it the right one?'

'It will be best if you think so.' His eyes glinted with that hidden laughter again.

She tried not to glare at him as she nodded towards the gargoyle. 'So what will you do with that?'

'I shall place it where all trapped demons are kept,' he said. 'On the roof of the church, where it will weather away until it is nothing.'

'No!'

Both Pam and Dunkley turned. They saw James covered in mud, sitting entangled in string.

'Turn it back. Pam tell him! Our Granny taught me how to summon it! What about my tomatoes?' he wailed.

'Use fertilizer from the garden center, like everyone else.' Carrying the new gargoyle, Dunkley shut the gate behind him.

Rain Stopped Play

'Look at that wheat field.' Trewithick, his blond hair caught back in a sensible ponytail, made a broad gesture. 'It's almost unharvestable with all those crop circles.'

Dunkley stirred his tea, looked away from the annual cricket match—students vs. lecturers. Both he and Trewithick wore cricket whites, waiting for their turn at the crease. They sat, watching the rest of the match, on the outside smoking terrace of the Cricket Pavilion.

'Odd, I agree,' he said. A faint Scottish accent scratched at his throat. 'We're in limestone country, not far from the cave where they found that prehistoric art. But this *is* an earth circle.'

Trewithick sat up straight, staring at the stone circle surrounding the cricket pitch, hired for the day by the college. The stones were squared off, but not capped like Stonehenge.

'Have you checked? We could be sitting on top of an elemental. It would have to be huge to spawn all those little ones.'

'I never check earth circles,' said Dunkley. 'Earth elementals are too rare. Stone Age man hunted them for...'

'Save the lectures for them.' Trewithick nodded to where the students had just taken another wicket. 'Who's next to bat?'

Dunkley balanced his cup and saucer on the rail surrounding the terrace and fished the list up from the floor at his side. 'Kilbride, then you're next.'

Dropping the list onto his knee, he picked up his cup and removed the teaspoon. He sighed. 'Can I borrow your lighter?'

Trewithick looked over and saw a long hair dangling from the spoon.

'A hair to bind around your heart. One of the oldest charms there is,' said Trewithick. 'It's almost as long as your hair. Are you sure it's not just one of yours?'

'It's dyed, with henna.' Dunkley flicked his waist-length plait of brown hair over his shoulder.

Trewithick laughed as he dug into his pocket. 'It should go out on the College Prospectus, *Mothers of students at the College are reminded that Alasdair Dunkley is married to his career.* Which one is it this year?'

'Daphne Green.' Dunkley's nostrils flared. 'I don't know which of us is more embarrassed, David or me. He's taken his laptop and is working by your field of circles.'

'So he doesn't have to watch his mother's fruitless assault on the impregnable fortress? Stop teasing the poor women by being so stand-offish.' Trewithick produced his cigarette case and a silver plated lighter. He tossed the lighter to Dunkley, who fielded it and held it under the strand of hair.

The hair shriveled with the heat and he let the burning remains fall into an ashtray. The cup of tea, he tipped into the aspidistra that led a lonely existence on the terrace.

'Now you've done it.' Trewithick accepted the return of his property. 'That poor plant is going to be in love with Daphne Green.'

'Better it than me. She lives here in Ackerton,' Dunkley said. 'The plant will see her sometimes.'

'Oh yes, I forgot,' Trewithick said. 'It was David Green, who suggested this place as a good site, wasn't it? I think a cricket pitch within a stone circle gives our match a proper ambience for the Theological College of St Van Helsing.'

Dunkley glared at Trewithick. 'Do you have to perpetuate that ridiculous nick-name?'

Trewithick grinned. He looked around, guiltily, before opening his cigarette case. He didn't offer one to his friend—it only would be refused. Dunkley wafted away the smoke.

Putting his case and lighter back in his jacket pocket, Trewithick produced a string with three knots tied in it.

'Try this, it's another old charm.' He tossed the toy over.

Dunkley's face brightened as he studied the little charm. 'I didn't think anyone made these anymore.' He untied the first knot and a gentle breeze blew the smoke back towards Trewithick.

'I'm from Cornwall, remember? Every fishing boat, whether it has sails or not, has one of these pinned up in the bridge. Your David Green has been asking me about them.'

Dunkley pulled a sour face. 'I wish he wasn't mine. Which idiot on the college council decided putting a state school boy, who hates anyone who went to public school, with me?'

'Don't ask me,' said Trewithick. 'However, I would appreciate your opinion on whether that charm-maker needs investigation. It's quite a strong elemental to be captured that way... What the hell is that?' He stood suddenly.

Dunkley looked up from the little wind charm to see a massed crowd of men jostling their way up the road.

'A pitch invasion?' he suggested. '"Do they have pitchforks?" is the most important question.'

'Ha ha, very funny.' Trewithick stubbed out the cigarette in the ashtray and leaned over the balustrade. 'Green!'

A student looked up from his laptop. Noticing Trewithick's gesture toward the crowd coming up the lane, he jumped to his feet and rushed back to the pavilion. He arrived at the rail panting.

'But that happens on May Day by the old calendar, not May the first. Mother?' He scrambled onto the terrace, over the balustrade as Trewithick and Dunkley stepped back.

Daphne Green must have been waiting outside the door. She opened it and walked onto the terrace, looking hopefully at Dunkley.

He ignored her.

The aspidistra's leaves managed to brush her shoulder as she came over.

'David, what is that?' Dunkley asked.

'It's the annual football match between Ackerton and Metherby,' said David. 'But they play it on May 13th not May 1st. Mother, what's happened?'

'It's too vexing.' Daphne tried to talk only to Dunkley. 'The Parish Council decided at the last minute to change it to May 1st because they wanted to attract American Tourists and Americans use the new calendar. We've even got sponsorship from a computer company this year.'

'The calendar only changed in 1752,' muttered Trewithick. 'I suppose we have to use the new one eventually.'

'But the Ackerton goal is the stone altar in the circle. They'll have to go right over our cricket match to get there,' David wailed. 'Or worse, through that field.'

Out on the pitch, play had suspended to watch the surging crowd. The mob now jostled back the way it had come.

'Metherby must have the ball now,' said David. 'Maybe it'll go all the way to the millstone at Harlton Cross Mill.'

'Dave! That's a fine thing for an Ackerton boy to say,' his mother said.

Trewithick frowned at the scrum on the road. People were climbing on the hedges and gesticulating wildly. With a splash one fell into the beck. A huge roar of laughter rippled through the mob as the story was passed along.

Daphne wrung her hands. 'Oh get out on this side, do. Mr. Cleats has forbidden the match to go through his lands.' She waved at the field where Trewithick had noticed all the crop circles. 'Oh no! The ball is coming back this way.'

'Green, you come with us,' Trewithick said. 'I think we need to go and look at the football match and see if it can be diverted around us. Tell me about this game, please. It doesn't look like football to me. Too many people for one.'

Trewithick vaulted the balustrade to the ground.

Dunkley retied the first knot in the charm string and put it in his pocket before following him down.

Dave swung carefully over and dropped to join them.

Dunkley barely kept the scorn off his face at the cautious approach. 'You need to spend more time in the gym. You were telling us about this football?'

Dave sniffed. 'It's the whole of Ackerton against all of Metherby. It's another of these fertility rites, I think.'

'I know the ones,' said Trewithick striding across the pitch. 'The aim being to shed blood on the ground to ensure fertility of the soil. A ritualized battle, that sort of thing?'

'Yes,' said Dave. 'Every farmer wants the ball to touch his land.'

'So why isn't Mr. Cleats interested?'

Dave looked guiltily at the fence. 'Some people like to think they are modern. He was one of the trial farms for GM crops.'

'Ah! That would explain the profusion of circle spoor,' Trewithick said. 'Greater use of the concentrated man-made fertilizers encourages new earth elementals.' He looked up as the umpire ran over to speak to the senior lecturers.

'Are we going to have to cancel, sir?'

'We're just going to check. It might be time for a tea break,' Trewithick said.

By the time they reached the lane, the mob had jostled back down it.

Dunkley removed his white cricket shoes and socks and turned up the hem on his perfectly ironed white trousers. He paddled across the beck and climbed on the fence, balancing with his feet on either side of a post.

On Farmer Cleats's land he saw group of five men in suits, sipping cocktails sitting comfortably in a wagon with a banner advertising their computer firm.

They must be the sponsors David mentioned, he thought and returned to watching the game.

'So what do you see?' shouted Trewithick.

'It looks more like a rugby scrum,' said Dunkley. 'The ball's gone into the river now, just where this beck joins it. There are about a dozen people jumping in for water polo. The rest of the scrum is fanning out along both banks and over the bridge.'

Dave spoke up. 'Those men specialize in water play. The ball can get all the way to the Metherby goal, the Mill stone's at the river edge.'

'Yes, but do *we* have to stop?' asked Trewithick.

'I don't know… I can't see the ball in play,' said Dunkley. 'Ah! It's coming up the beck.'

The ball flew through the air towards him.

He caught it, but it unbalanced him. He chose to jump, still holding the ball, rather than lose dignity by falling.

As he landed in the field, the earth seethed around his feet.

Dunkley quickly regained his balance as the mob surged back up the lane towards their ball.

Dave shouted, 'Throw it back in the river. Then we can get on with our game.'

Dunkley was about to toss it into the mass of men, when he looked at the post. He frowned, then inspected the churning soil. He put the ball down between his feet and yanked something off the post. Then, with a determined look on his face, he picked the ball back up and climbed over the three bar fence, paddling back over the river.

Behind him, the ground continued to swirl violently.

Dunkley tossed the ball to the crowd that was surging up the road. It bounced on the tarmac and rolled towards the mob.

'Someone has those earth elementals contained in that field like battery hens.' He showed Trewithick what he had taken off the fence, a tattered version of the string he had given him earlier.

'You shouldn't have taken the restraint,' said Dave. 'They're getting out.'

Dunkley smiled at the breakout. 'I don't understand why they were contained. They're not doing the crops any good in that profusion.'

'But they're getting out,' shouted Dave, pointing for emphasis.

Dunkley studied the churning tidal wave of earth flowing out of his breach in the fence. It dammed the beck and water spilled out and down the road. He watched for about two seconds then snatched up his cricket shoes.

'Run!' he shouted.

Trewithick had already made the same assessment. He was halfway back to the stone circle enclosed cricket pitch. Dunkley grabbed Dave by the wrist and pulled, but Dave hung back.

'You've got to put them back,' he shouted. 'You let them out.'

'This is no time for you to suddenly become brave,' Dunkley shouted.

Dave wrenched his wrist free and scrambled across the disintegrating dam. His feet slipped in the moving soil. At one point he had to pull his foot from where it had been buried to the ankle. Once on the other side of the dam, he jumped onto stable ground. Climbing the fence at the nearest post he wrenched a string from where it was nailed.

The five men with suits that Dunkley had seen watching the football match from a wagon in the forbidden field came running. Each one of them yanked a twist of string from a post and climbed over the fence.

As Dunkley watched them, the earth split around him. The elementals separated and escaped. The earth shook more frantically as the ones still trapped tried to get out before the would-be heroes got into place. Another huge surge of earth knocked out a whole section of the fence.

Dunkley turned and ran. More waves of earth poured out of the field.

'Earthquake!' one of the football players yelled.

The mob panicked. Screams sounded as the first wave of earth tipped the front ranks.

The tarmacked road cracked and buckled as the elementals fled their confinement. The dammed beck flooded in all directions.

From inside the stone circle, the college watched the show. Dunkley hurdled the bank. He landed and rolled down into the internal ditch of the henge. Flat on his stomach, he peered over the top of the bank.

As one, the students and professors joined Dunkley in his place of relative safety. He looked over the edge of the bank watching the events below.

'Knowing when you're out-matched,' he said to the nearest student, 'and when to run is one of the finer parts of our job.'

The student nodded at this wisdom. Trewithick, who had run at the first suggestion, skidded to the ground next to Dunkley.

'What the hell is that little fool of yours doing?'

'I have no idea,' said Dunkley. 'He has never shown any hints of bravery before this.'

Trewithick jumped up. 'NO!' he shouted, desperately. 'Not the third knot!'

The skies darkened as he shouted. He ducked back down. The waves of earth elementals stopped, then started flowing back.

'Released the air elementals bound in the strings, have they?' Dunkley asked.

Two different types of elementals, mortal enemies, met.

Dunkley got to his feet as the six freed air elementals and the mountains of earth elementals churned into a tornado in their fight for supremacy.

Trewithick caught hold of Dunkley's arm. Dunkley crouched to hear him as the howling gale increased crescendo.

'Where are you going?'

'I'd better get them out of there.'

Trewithick shook his head. 'I thought you said that anyone who gets himself into a situation had better be able to get himself out?'

Dunkley grimaced. 'I'm not trying to save the idiot boy. It's the young earth elementals. There may be sixty or so of them, but they'll never last against six mature air elementals.'

A hailstone hit the ground near Trewithick. Then another. A mass of ice pounded the ground as if the sky was falling. The cricket teams charged into the pavilion. Trewithick rolled underneath the front steps, followed by Dunkley.

'Can you activate the circle?' Trewithick shouted over the drumbeat.

Dunkley lifted an eyebrow.

'God, man! This isn't the time to work to rule, can you bloody activate the bloody circle?' he shouted.

'I know the theory,' Dunkley hedged.

'I thought you might,' Trewithick said.

'Why do you want the circle activated?'

'You said this is an earth circle, it would hold the earth elements safe while we chase off the air ones.'

'I'd need a few things. The kitchen might have them.'

He ducked out from under the steps and dashed out.

A hailstone the size of a cricket ball caught him in the shoulder as he charged up the steps and in the front door. Slamming the door behind him, he grimaced.

'Mr. Dunkley,' a voice shrilled.

He wiped his face clear again before turning to face Daphne Green. He nodded at her. 'Mrs. Green, I'm afraid I'm a bit busy right now.'

'Oh Mr. Dunkley,' she clung to his arm. 'You've got to save us.'

'I'd be working on that quicker if I didn't trip over you every time I turn round,' he muttered. Dodging around the crowd in the pavilion entrance hall, he pulled Daphne Green into the kitchen and firmly shut the door.

'Right, Daphne.' Dunkley forced a smile. 'You need to sit down for a while. Here, I'll make you a cup of coffee.'

He turned, knowing that she watched his every move through rosy-glasses. He would never understand this obsession that women felt for him.

He boiled the kettle and made a cup of coffee for her. Checking his watch, he stirred it anti-clockwise.

'Here, Daphne, drink this,' he said.

She sipped the coffee. 'This is very kind of you Mr. Dunkley.'

'That's all right, Daphne.'

'Gosh that's very odd coffee.' She yawned.

'That's because it was anti-coffee.'

Daphne Green frowned, then yawned again. 'What's anti-coffee?'

'It happens when you stir coffee widdershins. Coffee makes you wide awake, and more able to concentrate; anti-coffee makes you more pliable and sleepy.'

He pulled a penknife from his pocket. The handle was worn. Then he changed his mind and plundered the buffet. Picking up a plastic knife he held it out, handle first.

'Take this knife, with no return of gift, to cut the love. Now, you will sleep,' he said, his voice echoing from the ceiling of the kitchen block. 'When you awake this will all be a ridiculous dream. Why would any woman chase after a man like Alasdair Dunkley?'

With her hand fisted around the knife handle, she laid her head on the table. 'I have to get Dunkley in love with me, so he doesn't suspect. We have to keep the elementals contained,' she mumbled, 'for the money.'

'Stay in a trance, but answer questions,' he ordered. 'Tell me about making money from elementals.'

Daphne sat up straight, her eyes glazed from the sleep charm. 'We sell them to the computer industry.'

'What use does a computer company have for elementals?'

'They tell me that a suspension of iron alloys makes good memory storage.'

'So you are battery breeding the elementals for slavery? Have I got that right?'

'We need the money.' Daphne shrugged. 'It's not like they are people. It's not slavery.'

'Go to sleep,' Dunkley spat. 'Forget this business with earth elementals.'

Obediently, her head dropped to the table.

Clenching his fists, Dunkley returned to the buffet table and grabbed activators for the circle: some bread and cheese, and a box of wine. Above him, he heard the hailstones cracking the wooden tiles on the roof of the pavilion. He added two metal trays to his haul.

Re-entering the corridor, he saw the students and staff gathered to cheer him on.

'Going to sort it out now, Dunkley?' Kilbride asked.

'I'll have a go,' he said. Lifting the tray over his head, he ducked out into the storm and back to where Trewithick waited under the steps. He shoved the trays ahead of him.

'Right,' Trewithick said. 'Can you really do this?'

'The application of gifted and inherent Cræft is very similar. It's just that using inherent power exhausts us.'

'I haven't followed a word of that,' Trewithick said. 'Save it for your Advanced Theory class.'

'The Council would have me up for heresy if I taught our gentlemen that sort of thing,' Dunkley said. 'Here's your shield.'

'I can do anything that's needed from under here, thank you.'

'You will banish the air elementals, while I hold the earth safe.' Dunkley grinned. 'And you can't contact air elementals with your belly hugging the ground.'

Trewithick snarled. He tugged the tray over to him and wriggled out from under the pavilion.

'Oh yes,' Dunkley added. 'And what I was trying to say was, be prepared to pick up the pieces of me when I keel over with a heart attack from attempting the impossible.'

Trewithick continued out into the storm.

Moments later, Dunkley followed. With the tray over his head, he sprinted to the stone altar that stood at the north end of the stone circle.

Behind him, dirt gray clouds tumbled out of the sky as the tornado spun in ever more furious circles. Huge hailstones pounded the ground, tearing divots of grass from the pitch. The ground twisted up in a vast dust devil. Over the roar of the unnatural storm he heard the screams of the erstwhile footballers.

Dunkley crouched on the lea of the rock, balancing the tray over his head. The hail tinged the metal tray was distracting, but it was that or be knocked out.

As he turned the tap on the box of wine, filling an indentation in the rock, he hoped that Trewithick would not feel it necessary to inform on him to the Council. He laid out the bread and the cheese as offerings. Looking around he snatched a handful of daisies, scattered them around the bread and cheese then ducked back under his tray.

Taking a deep breath, he pricked his finger with the old penknife. His blood dripped into the wine.

The circle was old. The last activation had been an age ago. Now it lay sleeping. Dunkley called to the latent power trapped here, hoping that this wasn't one of the circles used to hold a demon so strong that it was unkillable. At least this was a single circle—not a double, or even the triple ring use for such creatures.

He felt no presence, but an elemental that powerful could mask its location from him.

The circle's power flowed sluggishly, the working pulling strength from him.

The little elementals fought the summons. There were too many of them. But he called them until the sun and sky spun into darkness.

A warm spirit filled his mind. *You have returned.*

'I beg your pardon?' That was not what Dunkley was expecting. 'What are you doing here? You're not bound.'

I chose to hide, in this welcoming place, from the little people who want their red paint from our corpses for their pictures in the heart of the Earth.

This made sense to Dunkley. 'Am I like someone you knew from before? Is that why you think I am returned?'

He felt a rough hand brushing his brow.

Ah! I am mistaken. This is your first visit. Why do you bind the young?

'I'm trying to save them from air,' Dunkley said.

21

I can gift you with the strength to call the young.

'No! I take no elemental gifts. I am your enemy.'

Not yet, but I am not bound by your illusion, Time; I see the future, the warm spirit said. *You could be the enemy of all sentient beings should you unwisely accept a gift from my kind.*

'That will be never.'

Never is too uncertain at this point—there are always good reasons for accepting a gift. Rest. I will give the young safety.

The warmth left him. The chill hail stung his back, waking him from the dark. Lifting his head, he looked out on Hell.

The earth in the circle exploded in a mud volcano, engulfing the twirling, twisting tornado that was six air elementals. Dunkley curled into a ball, trying to hide behind the altar stone.

The wind howling through the stones.

The earth thundered, as quake after quake ripped through the rock that lay under the fertile soil.

Then he was the soil, hard rock broken by the wind and water.

He called on the sun to bring the tree roots that stopped the wind and the water from washing him into the sea.

No! He clung to Dunkley. He would not be possessed by any part of the elemental experience.

From his pocket the air elemental begged to be freed. It could stamp on the earth that threatened his life and sanity.

Dunkley snatched away the hand that was already acting to draw the string from his pocket.

'NO!' He shouted into the turmoil. 'I want calm now.'

Pushing up on the altar stone he stood and spread his arms to the sky.

'There will be calm now!' he shouted into the wind. His face as still as a god carved from marble.

The raging world paused for a moment. In that instant, the six air elementals fled.

Remember that I obey, Master of Demons, said the earth spirit. *For when you visit again.*

The spirit of the circle slowly subsided back into its chosen containment. The young earth elementals sank into the land.

Dunkley lowered his arms. He saw Dave curled around a fence pole and people from the football game coming up to see if anyone had survived at the center of the maelstrom.

He sat on the altar. It was empty of the offerings. The storm striking from a clear sky had blown away the evidence of his awakening the circle—or the earth spirit had taken his gift.

In his pocket the trapped air elemental snarled. Dunkley crouched at the base of the altar, and scratched out a hole. He dropped in the knotted string and covered it with soil.

'Guard this for me, please,' he said.

The earth gave one last shudder as everything settled back to how it had been. The pounding hail turned into rain.

With a shaky hand, Dunkley tugged out his hip flask and took a sip of whisky. Trewithick, accompanied by a villager, charged over, his cricket whites spattered in dirt and debris. Dunkley looked down at his own mud and grass-stained clothes.

All things considered, it had not been a good day.

'Alasdair?' Trewithick said. 'Are you in there?'

Dunkley nodded; he took another sip from his flask. The ice-cold rain soaked him, but everything was calm.

'At least with the rain,' he said. 'We can call it a draw and stop getting trounced by the students.'

'What happened here?' the villager interrupted.

'The weather can get a bit odd around an earthquake, I understand,' said Dunkley. He forced a smile onto his face. 'Perhaps the countryside took exception to your changing the day of your annual football match.'

The Camera Just Piles on the Pounds

'Just act like a star-struck, stage-struck teenager,' Mr. Trewithick said.

While of course ecstatic to be asked to help by his teachers, Mike plodded from where they both remained in the car—up to the queue. He hunched his shoulders and jammed the tips of his fingers into his trouser pockets.

At the front of the queue, people rolled up sleeping bags and sipped from thermos flasks. Mike tried to suppress a sneer—it was amazing that anyone would camp all night just for this.

A girl ran up to her friend who stood next to Mike. 'Is my make-up right now? The mirrors in the ladies at the Underground are impossible!'

Her face looked plastic as she huddled with her friend under an umbrella, raised to protect their hairstyles from the few spots of rain. Noticing Mike, they eyed his tank-tee shirt and painted-on jeans.

'Want to come under?' the first one asked. The brolly barely sheltered the two stick-thin girls.

Mike flushed. 'I'm fine thanks.'

They gave his gym-fit body another once-over and giggled. He felt his flush darken, and yet he was wearing what amounted to the uniform for the boys in the line. Though most of them aspired to, rather than had, his physique.

At 8.30am the doors of the agency opened. A silence spread along the line as everyone craned their necks to see. Those who had arrived later than Mike peered around the corner, from where the queue now extended onto The Strand.

Two women emerged. They strolled down the line, comparing the candidates with images on their clipboards. Every now and then, they gestured someone indoors. The chosen one scurried down the steps into the basement offices of the Downstairs Modeling Agency. The unfavored ones remaining behind stared with open-mouthed envy. No one left, even after the selectors passed.

They stopped in front of Mike and scrutinized him. He studied them back. Both cast from the same mould, they exemplified everything these girls tried to copy.

'How would like to keep that figure without all the exercise?' Twin 1 said.

Mike blinked. His teachers were really hot on the subject of 'unfit people in our line of work don't last long'.

'Actually, I like working out at the gym,' he said. Well, learning antique weaponry was fun—the rest was a chore.

They pursed their lips, almost in unison. 'You like the discipline of hard work?' Twin 1 said.

Mike flashed a bright, insincere smile and said, 'Yes.'

'You sound like the sort we're looking for. What's your name?' Twin 2 asked.

He straightened. 'Mike Rider.'

Twin 2 held out her hand. 'Could I see your birth certificate, please? While you look about twenty, we are required to check that no one under sixteen slips through our selection process.'

Mike reached into his back pocket for his battered wallet. He unfolded it and shook out a square of paper.

'You're nineteen,' Twin 2 said. 'Good. I'm sure your attitude for discipline will translate into the maturity needed for this job. Go on in, please.'

Mike sauntered off.

An engine revved nearby, and Mike looked up hopefully, but it was a BBC van. The windows were darkened and a camera poked out the side window, trained on the crowd.

Mike sighed; then a wolfhound stuck its head out of a back window, lolling its tongue happily as it caught the breeze in its wiry fur.

A doorbell chimed twice in his pocket—the ringer set on his mobile phone —then it went silent. He relaxed.

A blonde teen-doll look-a-like caught up with him. Mike caught himself wondering if her breasts were implants, no one so thin had real gazongas that big and bouncy.

'Isn't this so exciting?' said the girl sucking in her stomach and flashing a toothpaste smile at the camera-car. 'Though I do wish they had waited until we were ready to be photographed. They say that a camera piles on the pounds. I bet we're on the news tonight. I'm Taylor.'

'Mike,' he said.

'Well, it's not really Taylor, but I looked through the fashion mags and thought I'd better use a modeling sort of name, don't you think?'

They descended into the basement. A tearful girl ran up the stairs and pushed them aside.

Mike watched her leave, then turned back to Taylor. 'I'll worry about names if they actually hire me.'

'Haven't you dreamt about this day all your life?'

Mike laughed—it just burst out. 'No, actually. I need a job to fund me through college.'

Taylor glanced at him warily. 'It's just like a reality show on the telly, isn't it?'

'We don't have television in my college Halls.'

That did it, Taylor skipped down the steps a little faster, away from a person so out of touch with Real Life. *I'm not with this weirdo*, her actions said.

You don't know how weird I am honey, he thought.

A tall man with a body to rival Mike's greeted them at the bottom of the stairs. He loomed at them, a faint smile drifting over his lips. His black suit, black shirt and tie, blending seamlessly with his black hair were designed to intimidate.

Taylor shrank away.

Mike gave him back look for look.

The tall man's thin smile became more genuine.

'Hi darlings, I'm Jason. You look like a Nordic couple to me,' he said. Over his shoulder, he added, 'Get them into ski clothes. We'll take their practice shots on the "ski run".'

'This way, kids,' sing-songed another woman with a clipboard. Mike christened her Twin 3.

Taylor pasted on a smile. Following her, Mike sneaked looks through doors, open onto the stark, whitewashed corridor.

The basement smelled damp and mildewy underneath the air freshener. Earlier candidates posed in unnatural positions for the camera, sucking in their guts.

'Oh I'll never be that thin,' Taylor whispered to Mike. 'I've dieted and dieted.'

Mike opened his mouth to contradict her, but Twin 3 looked over her shoulder. 'You don't have to worry about your diet. We have a nutritionist who will help you with all your… dietary needs.' She held open a door. 'There are clothes for you in that cubicle, girl. In that changing room for you, young man.'

Mike was faced with clothes that he had last worn on a skiing trip to Switzerland with school. They looked warm for July—thankfully the day was overcast. As he pulled up the zip on his jacket, he heard the other cubicle unlock.

'I've practiced the correct walk for weeks, after I read the ad,' Taylor said, her face red and glistening.

'Why bother?' Mike asked, thinking cool thoughts. 'If you read it, you'd know the advert said all training would be given.'

A door opened. Mike saw Twin 3 standing, listening to them.

Taylor wrinkled her nose. 'I wish I were partnered with someone more professional. Don't make me fail just because you can't be bothered. I'd do anything… I'd sell my soul to be a model.'

Mike's hand lifted to his neck and fingered the crucifix that his other teacher, Mr. Dunkley, had given him as he left the car.

'Just a precaution, Mr. Rider,' Dunkley had said.

Twin 3 looked at Mike as if waiting for a similar expression of enthusiasm.

He gave her a half smile and said, 'I'm sure I'll be able to prove my commitment to your satisfaction.'

Twin 3 nodded. 'Through here now, the photographer is ready for you.'

The skiing trousers they wore made swushing noises as they clumped after her in heavy ski boots. Mike looked around. A photo backdrop of an idealized pine forest, hung over a floor covered with a sheet and some polystyrene flakes. The flakes fluttered when people moved.

'Be a dear and make them up for me, will you?' said Twin 4, from behind a camera. She turned and rearranged some white umbrella arrays to diffuse the flashlight. Electric cables ran to a bank of sockets near the door.

How many of these clone women were there in this place? Now he thought about it, Taylor could almost be Twin 5.

Twin 3 checked Taylor's make up and passed it for the practice shoot. She dragged Mike to a table set up near the electrical sockets and flicked his hair into a wind blown style, holding it in place with hairspray.

'Now I need all mobiles turned off and put here,' she said, pushing aside some fashion magazines and dumping the can back onto the junk-filled table. 'And all your jewelry. We don't want any glinting on the camera. And that includes that chain around your neck, young man. It could slip out in an action shot and ruin the picture. When you've done that, get those skis fastened on. Hurry up about it.'

Reluctantly, Mike removed his neck chain and slid his mobile out from his pocket. He dumped them both on the table and quickly turned away to deal with the skis. He crouched and fastened the straps over his boots. He stood and slid the skis over the fake snow. Taylor looked awkward in the get-up.

'Hold your pole like this. And stand still or you'll trip over the skis.'

Taylor let him arrange her limbs. Then they stood on the fake ski slope, under the hot lights, pretending they weren't sweating.

For an eternity, they followed the directions shouted at them. The photographer and Twin 3 alternated giving orders with swigging from water bottles. Mike and Taylor eyed the water, bottled in the Strix region of Romania —the label held Mike's thirsty eye.

Eventually, it was over; they were told to await the verdict.

Twin 3 took Taylor aside and helped her off with the ski clothes.

Mike unfastened the straps on his skis. He watched everything. When Taylor had shed the skiing clothes, Twin 3 handed her a bottle of the water. Mike licked his dry lips.

'Now, you read this dieting manual,' said Twin 3, with a bright smile. She handed Taylor a book. Mike frowned. His mother's dieting books were all paperback with garish covers, not hardbound in pale-brown leather. Taylor opened the book hungrily.

Quickly, Mike set his skis and poles to one side and slid out of the waterproof trousers. He was unzipping his jacket, and wondering why Taylor merited a water bottle, when Jason entered the photo room with Twins 1 and 2.

Taylor rubbed her drooping eyelids, trying to look alert as she joined Mike.

'We loved you both,' Jason said. 'The photographer says you follow directions like a dream with no arguments. We'd like to hire you.'

Taylor squealed and hugged Mike. 'Thank you,' she whispered in his ear.

Awkwardly, he patted her back. But he saw Twin 3 whisper in Jason's ear. He flicked a glance at Mike, then nodded at Twin 3.

'I have your contracts here,' Jason continued. He waved the papers he held in his hand. Taylor's eyes followed the wafting paper as if it were a hypnotist's swinging watch. Mike looked longingly at the door—something felt wrong here.

'Look, after today I've changed my mind,' he said. 'Glad you got your contract Taylor.'

'Now wait a moment there, Mike,' said Jason. 'You said you needed help with college fees. This job is ideal—you work your available hours.'

Mike worried his bottom lip with his teeth. As long as he signed nothing, he should be all right. 'Okay, I'll look through the contract.'

'Oh darling, that's great,' said Jason. 'But first, our nutritionist needs to discuss your diet. We have strict requirements here, in this agency. We can make sure you never go hungry or get fat again.'

Finally he smiled, a proper toothpaste-grin baring his gleaming teeth. Around Jason, Twins 1 through 4 also smiled maniacally.

Mike saw the fangs.

His mind went completely blank. Beside him Taylor stepped forward, her eyes glazed over. Then he realized what he was seeing.

'Strix Water!' he screamed. 'Not Romania, Transylvania! You're infested with a vampire demon.' His hand went to his neck for his crucifix, which was... on the table behind the vampires. Twin 3's grin broadened.

Stepping slowly away from them, Mike grabbed Taylor's arm. 'Get behind me, I'll protect you.'

'What are you doing?' Taylor blinked dreamily.

'They want to infest you with a demon. They'll make you a vampire.'

Jason's eyes narrowed. 'Dear me! Have we a baby witch finder here? Sent to investigate us. Let's return him—with a present.'

The four Twins stepped forward, like chorus girls with a perfect routine. Mike retreated. He tried to remember anything he had learned about vampires this year—ever since he had accidentally signed on for a seven-year apprenticeship.

He continued backing up, trying to restrain Taylor from joining the kindred.

The twins' reaching hands became claws.

Mike broke, ducking away from Taylor.

A cable, hidden in the fake snow, tripped him and he tumbled headlong through the photo backdrop. He remembered to roll with the fall, but his back hit the wall, winding him.

Gasping, he scrambled to his feet in the tight space between the scene display and the wall.

Claws swiped long raking gashes through the backdrop.

He ducked right, but the claws left gouges across his cheek. He felt blood dripping down his chin.

Hunched over, he ran towards the door. The raking claws snagged in his jacket. More claws cut through in front of him.

He doubled back. If he could just reach the table!

Panic was going to get him killed, or worse. He had to think. *Right, let's see...* He wiped his chin and looked at the smear on his hand. *That's it! Vampires infested the blood. That made them water elementals.* He darted out into the room.

Fire opposes water. Mike snatched glances at the fittings. Surely fire-starting should be the first thing on the witch finder curriculum.

Moving with liquid grace, the four Twins pounced across the room.

He grabbed for Taylor's ski pole and swiped at the first of the fast-moving twin vampires, like he was using a quarterstaff.

The creature fell, burrowing into the fake snow. The other three blocked the exit. He had to move now!

He feinted for the door, then sprinted for the table, one of the twins on his heels.

He dived for shelter under the work surface, still clutching the ski pole, his only weapon.

The twin skidded to a halt and yanked out the chair. It clattered away.

As the twin vampire gripped the table, Mike got his feet raised and rammed up with all his force. It caught the vampire under the chin, jerking its head back. It flung backwards into another twin who tried to catch it, and they both dropped to the floor. The junk scattered everywhere.

Panting, Mike jumped to his feet. He *needed* fire, now! He ran a hand through his hair to push the strands out of his eyes and saw a can of hairspray. *The very thing.*

He snatched it up and slashed through the electricity cables with the spike on the ski pole.

Sparks flew into the volatile spray and the fashion magazines caught light. The flames flared into his face.

His eyes shielded by his arm, still covered in ski jacket, he kicked the burning mags into the photo backdrop and sprayed it with hairspray.

The backdrop slowly took flame.

Everyone in the room, bar him, shied away from the flames, even Taylor, who cuddled up to the leader, Jason.

Mike's heart sank—he'd abandoned her and they'd got her. Six feral stares turned on him. They promised death. Now what should he do?

He rubbed his dry lips and backed towards his fire. His foot knocked against his mobile. He ducked down, seized it and stabbed a number on his QuickDial.

It was answered, first ring.

'Mike?'

'There's bloody vampires in here,' he screamed, then added, 'Sir.'

'Dunkley, they're attacking him! We're on our way, Mike.'

Black smoke coiled up from where the fake snow was beginning to melt. The fire alarm blared through the building and the sprinkler system sprayed over the reluctant fire. With his toe, Mike scratched about in the junk on the floor for his crucifix. He kicked more combustible material onto his fire and emptied the hairspray canister into it, but the flames were losing the battle to the sprinklers.

Around him, the vampires edged ever-closer, restrained only by the dying fire.

The ringer on his phone chimed like a doorbell, alerting him to a text message. He flicked a look at the screen—it was from Dunkley. Darting glances at the stalking vampires, Mike scanned the message.

'Bll Bk Cndl Rd alwd.'

Bell! Right, thought Mike. He set his mobile chiming on repeat. Book! He skimmed the message. It was taken from the Book of Common Prayer; that was the Book! He would bet anything that Mr. Dunkley was texting from memory. Candle! He hunted for something he could use as a candle. The ski pole in his hand was carbon fiber. Carbon! Wood! It would burn.

He snapped the spike off over his knee and held the splintered end into the dying electrical fire, encouraging it to burn. It flared up immediately, his desperation adding the edge.

Feeling foolish, he lifted his burning skiing pole and wiped the misting water off his phone screen with a thumb. He read the words.

'*O Lord defend thy servants.*' His voice cracked, as the demons sent doubt his way. He cleared his throat and continued, '*That put their trust in thee. Send unto them help from above. And evermore mightily defend them.*'[1]

The body hosts of the Vampire demons screamed in pain.

His words drove the demons out of their hosts.

As water elementals, they dragged water with them.

The host bodies tried lapping water out of the air from the fire sprinkler system, desperate to re-hydrate. Even Taylor, who barely understood what was happening, was screaming with the pain of the creature that had taken her.

'*O Lord hear our prayer, and let our cry come unto thee.*'

His voice faltered to a halt as the hosts shriveled like sun-dried tomatoes. No one had mentioned what he should do now.

Out of their body-hosts, misty figures ghosted towards him through the fire-dousing spray. A gathering of water droplets formed into an arm reached for his nose, clearly intending to be drawn into his panting lungs.

He turned his head away, and pulled his tee shirt over his nose, trying to filter out the misty creature from his precious air.

The watery arm stretched down his shirt.

Mr. Dunkley and Mr. Trewithick burst through the door.

'*And for seven years the rain will fail and the rivers run dry,*' Dunkley said, glowering at the sprinkler system. The Scots burr in his voice sounded extra dry.

The water eased, then failed.

Mike felt the pressure of the demon rage lift as Dunkley took over the defense.

Mr. Trewithick looked like a demented angel with his blond hair flying loose from his ponytail as he stood in front of Mike. '*Then a great fire rushed through, but the Truth was not in the fire.*'

Mike's pitiful fire leapt eagerly up. It grew up the backdrop like a vine. The misty water elementals crowded away from the heat.

'Get out of here,' Trewithick shouted to Mike.

Mike needed no second warning; he paused only to pick up Taylor. She clawed at her face from the pain, trying to swallow with a parched throat, but

---

[1] Taken from the 1662 Book of Common Prayer.

she was not shriveled. He had driven the demon out of her before she had been properly possessed.

As he ran up the steps to the street, Mr. Trewithick and Mr. Dunkley shouted more excerpts from the Book of Common Prayer over the sound of the fire alarm.

Dunkley's two wolfhounds sat at the entrance, sniffing everyone who fled the fire. They growled a little at Taylor, but Mike pushed them away.

As he carried her lightly into the street, he could hear fire engines' sirens wailing down The Strand. Dunkley and Mr. Trewithick quit the burning building. Mr. Trewithick closed the door. Dunkley ran over to Mike.

Mike crouched and lowered Taylor to the pavement. She slapped him across the face.

'You bastard, you stopped me from become the next supermodel.'

Mike shied away. 'But they were turning you into a vampire. It's how they keep thin.'

'Vampires! That's nonsense! I was being told dieting secrets and you burned down the Agency. Are you a Religious Nutter or something? I heard you spouting that God stuff.'

Dunkley rubbed the soot from his close-trimmed beard. His eyes twinkled, but he set his face into pious constipation. 'Yes, we are Religious Nutters, here to save you from the depravity of that life.'

'He was going on about vampires. Stories!' Taylor spat.

'Yes,' said Dunkley, the Scots accent promised Hellfire, but Mike could see his lips trying not to twitch into a grin. 'Evil Vampires that suck the health and vitality from today's youth, forcing them into the shallow life of celebrity.'

'He said you didn't have television or anything. You really are a Nutter.' She pulled away from him and wept into her hands.

'But I rescued her,' Mike muttered. 'Why did you tell her that stupid stuff? She thinks we're—that I'm crazy now.'

'That's the way it is in our career,' said Dunkley. His wolfhounds snuffled his hands. 'Did you expect to get the girl and ride into the sunset with her on your white charger? I told her what a normal person could believe. We are— you are—set apart from them now.' His hazel eyes reflected the fire behind them.

'I think we can pass you into year two, Mike,' said Mr. Trewithick, wiping his glasses on his shirttail as he joined them.

Mike spun to look at Mr. Trewithick, his mouth dropping open. 'You mean all of this.' He waved a hand at the burning building. 'All of this was just my end of year exam?'

'Well, we could hardly test your practical skills with multiple choice questions, now could we?'

'If it's any consolation.' Mr. Dunkley flicked Trewithick a quelling look. 'We thought we had sent you on an observe-and-report assignment. I didn't expect it to blow up in your face like that.'

'But what about her?' Mike pointed at Taylor, who lay weeping on the pavement.

'Yes,' said Mr. Trewithick. 'I'm afraid we had to take marks off you because you let her get infested. It stopped you getting a distinction. Now, can we give you a lift back to your Halls of Residence?'

'This is all just a game to you, isn't it? Don't you care at all about the people you rescue?' Mike shouted with his nose level with Mr. Trewithick's. 'You two could have waltzed right in and sorted it without my aid.'

His hand still clutching the broken, burnt ski pole rose almost by itself.

Mr. Trewithick replaced his glasses and calmly regarded his student.

Mike looked at the pole then flung it at the doorstep of the burning modeling agency. Without looking back at the sobbing girl, he strode to the car.

Dunkley slid open the back door of his people carrier. He nodded at the ski pole.

'Excellent improvisation with non-standard equipment by the way, Mr. Rider. Come, boys.'

His wolfhounds jumped into the car.

'From Ghasties, and Ghoulies, and Long-Leggit Beasties...'

On the television screen, the News camera displayed the yew trees dripping, with late summer rain. The stone church guarded the left of the picture and at the open church gate stood an ambulance and two police cars with blue lights strobe over the scene.

The full moon shines down on where something has been digging at the newly filled grave. Dunkley surveys the claw marks. Hefting his wolfspear, he feels a moment's relief—they tell him that the infestation is new. The creature is hungry, but has not—yet—learnt to hunt.

Two wolfhounds snuffle at the scrapes. Calmly, Dunkley checks around him. The yew trees cast shadows that shift in the breeze. Lit from inside by the glorious moon, luminescent clouds drift across the sky. Pure white, like the white coating on the blade of the wolfspear.

The night is not cold, but he turns up the collar on his biker jacket and zips it over his throat. He lifts a bottle from his pocket. It looks like an ordinary drinking bottle, but he uses it to squirt nearly a complete circle near the grave. A pinch of salt and a bishop's blessing make this water holy: salty, like the compassionate tears of a Savior.

From his side, Rory growls.

Dunkley turns sharply, his long plait of hair swinging out, his wolfspear at the ready. A large manwolf hurls from the cover of the yew trees.

Snarling, Ross charges the beast while Rory crouches, ready at his master's side.

The creature leaps over the dogs and straight at Dunkley.

He ducks down, the wolfspear raised.

The creature sees the spear. Twisting and frantically lashing its tail, it tries to change direction mid air. The tip of the spear catches the creature's inner thigh.

It howls in pain, a long aching note not heard in Britain for four hundred years. The creature cuts and runs. Clearly visible in the quiet, midnight light, it leaps over the church wall.

Calling his dogs, Dunkley follows. One hand braced on the top, he vaults the wall. His boots beat down on the tarmac road as the moon glints off the white spear tip.

Silver may be traditional, but there is a better catalyst, which is why Dunkley always edges his wolfspears in platinum.

The hammer clangs on the hot metal. The red light from the firebox drowns the daylight coming in through the open door. With arms bare in the heat of the forge, Dunkley brings down the first blow, the telling blow that will show him if the metal will produce the temper he looks for in a blade.

The cold moon glares down, her hawk-bright eye on the creature running through the village. The houses, friendly cottages in the sun's warm, forgiving light, at night loom over a street plunged into shadow by the moon's stark, black and white beliefs of right and wrong.

Her pure light exposing the affront to nature, she lights the trail for Dunkley.

Rory and Ross alternate between running ahead to sniff the path and trotting close, ready to protect their master. A slow jog, Dunkley puts one foot in front of the other. This could be a long run.

Raw from the fire, the red-hot bar flattens under repeated blows. His arm holds to the steady rhythm needed to create a true blade. For strength and springiness, he folds a bar of carbon steel into the center of the wrought iron and seals it inside with hammer blows.

The others tell him to use a gun, that the chase is unkind. What they mean is that they do not wish to put themselves to the trouble of chasing. Dunkley knows that the silver bullet in a gun kills the body host as well as the wolf demon. If there is the smallest chance to save the person who was infested, he must take that chance, whatever the danger to himself.

The flattened bar has cooled and he stokes the fire in his furnace.
The bellows blow the glowing coals brighter.
Carefully, he chooses the place into which to thrust his metal again.

The creature lives in this village—Dunkley knows that. Hereabouts, there are family and friends who do not know what this creature becomes by the full moon; each of them is one more reason to save the host,

The pain of transformation drives it mad, as the body warps from man to manwolf.

Dunkley slows his pace. The creature knows every hiding place. He must lure or drive it into the open.

Ross charges.

The creature leaps out from behind the bin, knocking it over. The clatter echoes round the sleeping village.

An electric light flares in the house.

Both Dunkley and the creature freeze, then dive into cover, as the owner of the bin flings open his bedroom curtains. The sash window is raised and the bin owner glares at the scattered rubbish on his drive.

'Foxes!' he shouts over his shoulder. 'They should never have banned the hunt.'

The window slams shut. Dunkley sprints from his shadow, which is too close to the emptied bin. He hunkers down in a darker shadow nearer the street. The house door bangs open. Viciously tying the cord on his dressing gown, the man stalks out to clear up—and into danger.

Dunkley braces to intervene.

* * * *

He pulls out the red hot metal. For once the tongs fail to grip. The metal slides out of his grasp and towards his feet, but the shock of meeting the cold floor could ruin the blade. Dunkley jumps out of the way. The flattened bar clatters dully on the stone floor of his forge. He leans down with his tongs and retrieves the metal bar. He thrust it back into the fire—the next round of beating into shape will show him the finished work.

Where is the creature? As he moved away from the house, Dunkley lost sight of the manwolf.

He squints into the darkest corners, it has to be here. Even Dunkley can smell the food in the split plastic bags.

Then Dunkley can see it, creeping one limb forward at a time. It is quivering, barely holding back from rushing the plastic bags.

The man bends over, his back to the creature. As he sweeps the scattered rubbish into his dustpan, his curses, of the namby-pamby government that banned fox hunting, cover any noise the creature makes as it stalks the rubbish.

The wolfhounds crouch, ready to distract the creature. Dunkley is poised to spring with the wolfspear ready. The smell drags the creature into the open. One thrust of its powerful hind legs and the manwolf lands beside the man, knocking him aside in its desperation to get at the sweet smelling food.

The creature howls that long note. Its teeth rip open the plastic to get at the carcass of the Sunday chicken.

The man cries out in pain as his head slams against the wall. The sharp edge of a stone block cuts into his head. Dazed, the man lifts his hand and looks at the red stain on his fingers. His eyes are wide and white with fear as he sees this thing from nightmares inhabiting the waking night.

The smell of fresh blood awakens something in the creature. It growls low and bares its fangs. Its eyes lock onto the man. Snarling, it slinks towards him.

The man curls up behind raised hands, ducking his chin, protecting his throat from those ice white teeth.

Dunkley is there.

The wolfhounds each sink fangs into a hairy leg, dragging at the creature.

It half turns and rakes its claws down Rory's back. Grimly, the hound holds on.

The creature howls again, this time in pain. Dunkley spears its shoulder.

The burning, platinum-edged blade sets the wolf demon inside the body-host reeling. One wolfhound nips at the manwolf's throat, the other rips at the injured arm.

He withdraws the bar from the heat and inspects it. It seems right, but the shaping will tell. He turns the flattened bar on its side and begins the rhythmic pounding again, forming the bar into a classic leaf shape. The blade is too short to be a sword. It is too curvy to be a knife. He beats out a point.

* * * *

Driven by the pain, the creature backs away from the injured man, swiping with huge clawed hands at the hounds that harry it.

Without another look at the man on the ground, Dunkley jumps over him to where the dogs herd the creature into the shadows.

Still sniffing towards the enticing scents of the bin, the creature flees the snapping dogs and the dreadful spear.

Dunkley halts a moment and runs a hand over Rory's back. The hound licks the scrape—it is superficial. Rory wags his tail and gruffs, ready to continue the chase.

Dunkley's heavy boots pound the road again. Behind him, fading into the night, he hears a door slam shut.

More heating. Dunkley takes a glowing crosspiece from the firebox and, hammering on the hot metal, he welds it across the base of the blade.

At Town End Farm, the houses stop abruptly. Dunkley and the hounds jog into a lane. High hedges cast reaching shadows over the road. He whispers a word to his dogs and they sit, still alert. He listens intently for a moment then calls them on.

Ross takes the lead while Rory pads near Dunkley.

The height of the hedge falls and a gate through to a field halts them momentarily.

With a hand on the hinge end, and a foot on the lowest bar, Dunkley is over. Ross is quick to hurdle the gate in his wake, Rory scratches a way underneath.

Long grass swishes about his legs as Dunkley and his hounds follow the creature's scent. Then, at a beck, the scent ends. It's just a drainage ditch around a field really, but recent rains have filled it.

The moonlight shows the grass scuffed up where the creature slid down the bank into the muddy flow. Black streaks of the creature's blood stain the grass. The hounds snuffled up and down the bank, they cross over, splashing and churning up more muck from the bottom and do the same drill on the other side. The trail has gone cold.

For the next stage Dunkley holds an already flattened piece of metal into the fire. He hammers the heated bar around a metal form, producing a cone.

Heating both the blade and the cone he welds them, hammering the hot metal together. A stout ash shaft already rests against the forge walls. While it is still hot, he rams the socket of the leaf-shaped blade down over the ash—together they form a spear. Smoke curls up from the strong wood. A nail, driven through the socket and staff, secures the spear blade firmly.

Dunkley leans on his spear. Up or down. He watches the water as it begins to run clear over the drowned grass. He calls his hounds back and sets off up stream. As they walk, the dogs snuffle the edge of the water. Within minutes, they find another black stain on the grass where the creature climbed out. The dogs catch the scent again and start to run.

Long clouds crowd in from the north. The pure white clouds of earlier are tangled by the rising wind and the air takes on a chill. The moon will soon be gone. Dunkley picks up the pace. He can see the church from here. The dogs are leading him back to the graveyard.

Dunkley takes the now cool blade and sets the grind stone turning. He pulls a safety mask over his face and sparks fly around him as he sets the blade to the grindstone. Every so often he pulls away, lifts up the mask and checks the blade. Then he pulls down the mask and returns the blade to the stone.

He runs faster now. The dogs lead him around the edge of the field, not through the wheat awaiting harvest, a further sign—if he needed one—that the creature is local. Then his hounds lead him back to the churchyard.

Again he vaults the dry stone wall. His dogs scramble after him, their claws scrabbling against the rough boulders. He sprints into the shadow of the church and stealthily works his way around to where the fresh grave had been dug out. The manwolf is scratching at the ground with its good front pawhand, clawing away the soil from above the promised meal, before the rain arrives to cover the smell. It seems calmer now.

Dunkley slowly steps out of the shadow into the fading moonlight. His hounds fan out on either side.

The creature looks up.

'I can help you.' His confident tone fills the night. Again he produces the water bottle from his pocket. 'I have something here that will fill your hunger.'

The creature sniffs the air, but it can smell nothing. It limps forward on three legs—the front right is useless from the earlier mauling. It sees the spear and staggers back.

Taking a deep breath, Dunkley lays the spear aside and steps forward holding only the bottle.

'This will help you,' he says.

His soft Scottish accent seems to reassure the creature.

Dunkley keeps the circle he drew earlier between him and the creature.

Again the creature falters forwards. Its front paw drags.

Dunkley is sure that it cannot have fed for the three days of the full moon so far; it must be desperately hungry now.

It takes another step towards the ring.

Dunkley smiles holding the bottle in open hands. One more step and the creature will be inside the almost complete ring.

Finally a last check, the tip is sharp. He takes the spear to where he has set up an electroplating system.

He fixes the spear into a vice and lowers the blade to rest in the liquid. Switching on the system at the mains, he watches as the thin layer of platinum adheres, turning the blade matt gray then pure, tin white.

He switches off the system. He raises the blade from the liquid and frees it from the vice. He inspects the blade, taking pride in continuing the unbroken tradition from the Stone Age, when the wizard-smiths brought about the first industrial revolution, in their discovery of the magic of changing raw stone ore into bright metal.

Studying the spear, he can see that this one is good.

One more step.

The creature stops. It sniffs the air. It sniffs the ground. Then it lifts its head and howls in rage. The red, angry eyes lock onto Dunkley.

He lunges for his spear.

The dogs dart in from the side.

The creature leaps out from under the dogs—their claws scrabble in the loose soil, but they slide into each other, getting tangled.

The creature's claws rake Dunkley's leg, ripping through denim to tear into the flesh beneath.

Dunkley rolls away from the creature, but also away from the spear.

Lifting its pawhand, it licks the dark blood from its claws. It howls, turning sharply to finish Dunkley, but the wounded front paw gives under the strain and its muzzle bangs drunkenly against the ground.

The manwolf recovers as Dunkley scrambles to his feet.

The dogs circle the manwolf, looking for their next opening; they dart in, snapping at the rangy fur, as the creature turns this way and that, clawing and biting.

All the while it moves towards Dunkley. The slavering jaws open as it lunges.

Dunkley hurls the bottle into creature's maw.

It bites through the plastic and the liquid spills down its throat, burning the wolf demon from inside.

The creature howls again. It bats at its muzzle with the uninjured pawhand.

'I can help you,' Dunkley calls again.

The creature is too maddened to hear him. It leaps for Dunkley.

He dodges.

The creature turns, hugging its injured paw to its chest, and slams into Dunkley's side.

He is thrown into the wall of the church. Tucking in his chin, he avoids slamming his head into the wall. The hounds dart in, to drive the creature back. Dunkley pushes to his feet and staggers to where his wolfspear lies on the ground.

The creature tears away from the hounds and races him to the weapon.

Dunkley dives for the spear, rolling as he hits the ground. He grabs the haft as he rolls over it and up onto one knee. No time to stand, he braces the spear against his foot.

At the last moment the manwolf tries to turn aside but the wolfhounds snap at its back. The momentum forces the spear deep into the manwolf's chest. The dripping jaws snap millimeters from Dunkley's eyes, but the crosspiece holds the creature back.

A bitter sigh escapes its muzzle as Dunkley twists the spear. The carcass collapses at the knees, blood sputtering over Dunkley's clothes and boots.

The eyes are the last part to die. They change from angry red to surprised blue as Dunkley watches. The manwolf changes slowly back to a man. A naked young man—nearly a boy, no more than twenty—lies at the end of his spear.

Dunkley wrenches the blade free. He shuffles to the boy's side. His torn jeans rest on the fresh soil, scuffed by the fight and where the creature had been digging for meat to fill its hunger.

'I'm sorry,' whispers Dunkley. 'I am so very sorry.' He leans over and places a kiss on the boy's forehead.

For a long time Dunkley kneels in the dirt, knowing that this was another one he could not save. Dark clouds stretch out to cover the moon. Fat drops of rain splash onto the ribcage shattered by the wolfspear, but they cannot wash away the regret.

Ross lies down to rest, his tongue lolling; Rory licks the wound on his back. They both wait for their master.

With fingers bruised by the last rush of the creature onto his wolfspear, Dunkley pulls his wallet from an inside pocket of his leather jacket. He fumbles out a small rectangle of cardboard with only a simple cross printed on it. He fits the card inside the young man's hand.

Stiff and leaning heavily on his spear, Dunkley stands. He calls the dogs to heel, and limps out of the churchyard shutting the gate behind him.

The stretcher carried a body, with the face covered by a white sheet. A sobbing young woman, huddled in the arms of an older lady, followed behind. The detective in the picture fingered a white business card in his hand, then he slid it into his coat pocket.

A newsreader spoke in a voice over. 'In Wiltshire, the body of a young man was discovered near a partially re-opened grave this morning. The police are not looking for anyone else in connection with this incident.'

'...And things that go bump in the night, May the Lord and his Angels protect and keep us.'

Going for the Burn

'And what's this?' said a voice near Mike.

Mike growled under his breath. Distracted from watching the music video, he began to feel it as the machine increased resistance, as if pedaling uphill. He dragged his eyes from the video where a barely clothed girl cavorted about a chrome pole.

A man dressed in a suit sniffed at a plug-in air-freshener. His female companion, an employee of Health City club, answered the question with a practiced spiel.

'It's a special energizing mixture made up by our in-house Complementary Therapist, Annette Holgarth. I understand it contains extracts of nettle, ginger, rosemary, and milk thistle. And of course Ginseng, a very vitalizing herb.'

'It's a different scent in the changing rooms,' he observed.

'Oh yes,' the trainer said. 'In the changing rooms we have a lavender and chamomile mix, in order to calm the members' minds and bodies, getting them ready for the rest of their day.'

'I need to take samples.' He bent and plugged in his own machine, a red LED light flickered on, beating like a fly's heart. 'This will monitor the air quality in this environment.'

'Ms Holgarth has given her permission for this inspection,' the trainer said. 'But personally I think it's a waste of effort.'

'As I explained at the desk.' The suit spoke patiently. 'This is just a precaution. We have a link between this facility and a cluster of Post Viral Fatigue Syndrome cases.'

The trainer pursed her lips. 'We have a company policy, clearly stated in our membership guide, that people who have been ill, even if it's just a cold, should wait at least five days before returning to exercise. There are always those, so addicted to exercise, who pay no attention to this advice.'

They moved out of Mike's hearing range. His eyes snapped back to the siren on the screen, but the video had moved on. It now showed a woman singing in a meadow. The resistance was gone, as if freewheeling downhill. The readout said *cooldown*.

None of the other men on the horseshoe formation of exercise bikes around the video had looked up when the door opened. Feeling aggrieved at missing the best bit, Mike wondered if he could petition the college authorities to get plasma screens and music like this in the college gym. With one eye on Mr. Dunkley, working his arms on the weights, Mike remembered that not two hours ago he had been yawning through Mr. Dunkley's Ethics lecture for Third Years.

The door opened again and Mike's other teacher entered the room. He had a towel hung around his neck, but it looked unnecessary.

'Well,' said Mr. Trewithick. 'You have a better class of video in here. We had the financial news channel.'

'There was a better show five minutes ago,' Mike muttered as Mr. Dunkley joined them.

'Let's go, before the showers get crowded,' Dunkley said, 'I've found nothing. How about you?'

The rest of the young professionals were cycling through the cooldown of the exercise program Mike had been following. They looked close to collapse, but happy with it. Exercise addicts, that's what the trainer had said.

'Not a sausage,' said Trewithick. 'I'd say this place is clean. But it's always nice to try out new facilities.'

As he followed the two men, Mike wondered if he would ever manage that casual attitude to this job.

A ghost of a man had taken over at reception. He snatched a glance up as they passed through the entrance lobby to the changing rooms, but quickly returned to his viewing. Curious, Mike looked over the high desk and saw the man was glued to the music video that had been showing in the gym. His hand was poised, halfway between his mouth and the packet of raisins as the woman did her thing with the pole. The bit Mike had missed was next. He hovered, watching over the man's shoulder.

'Mike,' shouted Mr. Trewithick. 'Come on.'

Both teachers stood waiting for him. He hadn't even realized that they had walked off.

A breath of warmer air entered the lobby and Mike saw an older man hurrying over to lean on the desk.

'Is Annette available?' he whispered. 'I've got a date, I need to see her today.'

The receptionist looked up, blinking as if he was waking up. 'I'll check for you.'

He picked up the internal phone as Mike dragged his feet. He wanted to see that part.

'Oh hello Annette, Mr. Dassle would like to know if you have a free appointment today. You will?' He looked at the man, who was clearly a regular. 'Annette can see you right away, Mr. Dassle. If you'd like to go through.'

Unable to linger any longer, Mike joined his teachers.

'You think they'd put a better advertisement for the Health Club on the reception,' commented Dunkley. 'He looked like a stiff breeze would knock him over.'

'What was so interesting back there, Mike?' asked Trewithick.

'Nothing,' muttered Mike.

Now the guest passes were used, he would never see the rest of that video. There was no way his student loan would cover a membership to this place— most of the members worked in the financial district as stockbrokers.

'Can we hurry, please?' Dunkley said. 'I've got a tutorial to prepare for two o'clock and a history lecture for the ordinary college students at three. I'd like to eat lunch between now and then.'

'Sounds good to me,' Trewithick said. 'I've got to double mark some undergrad classics papers. At least this place isn't one for us.'

Mr. Dunkley might talk about teaching history to the ordinary students but to Mike he taught Advanced Theory and Mr. Trewithick taught Practical Applications.

'We're not the only ones investigating them,' Dunkley said. 'Mike, did you hear anything they said?'

Mike forced his mind away from his grudge.

'Those boxes he set up are air quality monitors,' Mike said. 'The air freshener does have a different scent in here, the suit was right.'

Both Dunkley and Trewithick automatically sniffed.

'Herbal,' Dunkley said.

'Lavender and chamomile,' Mike continued. 'The suit said there's a *cluster*, he called it, of Post Viral Fatigue caused by the Club. He took samples of both air fresheners.'

Mike looked away as both older men stripped to shower. It wasn't any form of coyness, just that the comparisons made him uncomfortable. Towering legends like Mr. Dunkley should be seven feet tall. *Or*, Mike thought, *at least looking me in the eye at 6'3*. Perhaps he should blue-eyed and angelically handsome, like Mr. Trewithick, whose blond hair was barely graying at forty.

Mike slipped into a shower cubicle.

'Can you remember the herbs in the gym air freshener?' Dunkley asked over the shower noise.

'Yes, sir,' said Mike, aware it was a test. 'It was nettle, rosemary, ginger, uh, ginseng, and milk thistle.'

'Ginseng? In an exercise room!' Dunkley sounded horrified. 'No wonder the men were panting over the videos of the dancing women.'

There was a smothered snort of laughter from Mr. Trewithick. 'Stop being such a prude, Alasdair.'

Mike was grateful neither of his teachers could see his blush—the dancer's moves still twirled in his head. When he emerged from the shower, Mr. Dunkley was already in the suit he thought appropriate wear for a college professor, working his waist-length hair into a plait.

A small screen ran advertisements for volcanic mud wraps and therapies to increase male vitality from the in-house Complementary Therapist. Mike thought that ten minutes in the gym watching the videos would help that problem. He tried to work out an excuse to return and watch the rest of the video.

Mr. Trewithick slipped his tie over his head and looked for a mirror to straighten it.

'Why aren't there any mirrors in here? Alasdair could I borrow yours?'

The advertising screen crackled a moment and Mike looked away. Dunkley tossed his divining mirror casually at Trewithick, who fielded it as if it wouldn't be bad luck if dropped.

After checking his tie, Mr. Trewithick finger combed his shoulder length hair into his usual ponytail. Mike's hair was still growing out of the short back and sides his mother had inflicted on him at Easter for his sister's wedding. Mike scrambled into jeans and a tee shirt.

'Ready yet?' Dunkley tied off his plait and looked around. 'Michael, that tee shirt's...'

Mike poked his head out of the neck hole and blinked. His mind was no longer filled by the images of the woman twirling around the pole.

'What's going on?' he asked.

Dunkley took two steps and put both hands on either side of Mike's head. He looked deeply into Mike's eyes.

'Now that's interesting,' said Dunkley releasing Mike's head. 'Why would anyone put a spell on young men? A simple spell at that, broken by the simplest counter charm of turning your shirt inside out.'

Mike looked at the frayed in-seams of his shirt.

'The video,' he said. 'You weren't watching it, sir, but all I wanted to do was sit and watch the video, like the receptionist.'

'Okay,' Trewithick said. 'So there's a spell in the videos, but what for?'

'Put it together, why don't you,' Dunkley said. 'The men who have Post Viral Fatigue, that male receptionist looking drained and worn.'

'The man who came in,' said Mike, interrupting the teachers. 'He was after something for a date tonight.'

'Let's go.' Dunkley fished his car keys out of his pocket. 'You go and sit in the car with my dogs, boy. This one isn't for you.'

Mike grimaced, one day Mr. Dunkley would remember he was twenty-one.

'Don't be silly, Alasdair. He'll probably be better off than you,' said Trewithick.

'On your head be it then,' Dunkley said.

It looked like they were needed after all.

The receptionist had returned to the video. Mike fought the desire to sneak another look at the screen. Instead he studied the posters discreetly advertising the services of the Complementary Therapist.

Dunkley looked tense but Mike knew Mr. Dunkley was never afraid of anything. Rumors around the college had Dunkley as pure as Galahad to fight the evil that the day brought.

'Where is the Complementary Therapist?' Dunkley demanded.

'She's with a client at the moment.' The pale young man took his eyes off the screen long enough to open a diary. 'If you'd like to make an appointment...'

Dunkley reached across, grabbing a handful of shirt he dragged the receptionist's ear down to his level. 'Now, tell us where the therapist is.'

A door opened behind the turnstiles and a man emerged carrying what looked like a prescription bag.

'She'll be through there,' Mike said. 'That man arrived as we left the gym.'

Trewithick neatly had the prescription bag off the man.

'Hey!' said the man. 'That's mine. I need it.'

Dunkley released the receptionist, who dropped to the floor and stayed there. Dunkley received the bag from Trewithick.

'*Man Up*? Well, that's subtle,' he said, reading the label on the bottle he pulled out. 'There's more than ginseng in here.'

Mike sniggered.

'Oh God!' said the man. 'Don't tell me it's illegal drugs! I didn't know. I just need a bit of a boost sometimes. It's not wrong to want a bit of help. You're drug officers aren't you?'

Dunkley said, 'We're going to need to keep this bag as evidence. If you can give your name and address to this young man, we will keep this as quiet as possible, sir.'

Mike found a piece of paper and swiped a pen from the desk as Dunkley and Trewithick stepped over the gaping receptionist.

He took the man's name and address.

'I'm not going to get into trouble for this am I?' said the client. 'You're too young to know what it's like to...'

Mike ignored the excuses. He pocketed the paper and went through the door and up the stairs beyond.

As Mike walked into the upper room he heard Mr. Trewithick saying, 'This *herbal supplement* is infused with vitality stolen from the young men downstairs.'

'You *church inspectors* are at the same liberty as the *health* inspectors,' said a female voice behind the door. 'You'll find nothing untoward.'

The woman sat at her computer with her arms folded. Next to her screen stood one of those silly little USB desk toys, this one was in the shape of a plasma ball. Further into the room, an incense burner released a thin spiral of smoke next to a treatment couch and a tranquil arrangement of brown and orange flowers stood on the windowsill.

Dunkley and Trewithick produced divining devices from their pockets.

Mr. Dunkley preferred to use a veiled mirror—he had his handkerchief already draped over the reflecting surface. Mr. Trewithick produced a small silver bowl and tipped a measure of brandy in from his hip flask. He added a few drops of oil and pretty colors swam about in the surface tension.

Mike stood at the door, studying their techniques.

The woman smugly watched the two men pace about her treatment room; their booted feet loud on the uncarpeted floor. Then she turned back to her computer screen with a simulation of unconcern. The plasma ball must be very sensitive as all the strands flickered to one side as the men walked past in their search.

Mike glanced down at the woman. The computer screen displayed lists of ingredients. She saved her file. Mike had a sudden twinge. He had no idea why, but he grabbed her wrist and prevented her clicking on shutdown.

'I'm not letting you steal my formulæ,' she screamed.

'We need to see those as part of the inspection,' Mike said.

As she struggled to free her wrist, her elbow tipped over a glass of something pink and carbonated. Liquid splattered over the table and dripped into the computer case below. It steamed and hissed, smoke poured out.

The glass rolled, knocking the plasma globe off the edge of the table.

'NO!' She dived for the ball of light, but it was too late. The glass shattered on the hardwood floor.

The tame lightning ball exploded through the room. Strands of plasma arced to touch every shiny surface.

Mike ducked under the table dragging the woman with him. Twisting her wrists, she broke his grip.

'Idiot boy,' she shouted, dodging his half-hearted attempt to rugby tackle her.

Lightning spilled out of the light socket. The light bulb exploded leaving the plasma strands as the only light in the room. They coalesced into snake-like strands of hair outlining a female figure, which stalked towards the woman who backed away.

The wooden floor smoldered under the creature's feet. Smoke from the trashed computer joined with the incense, they swirled and twisted under the lightning hair and filling in the picture of a staggeringly beautiful woman.

Mike hunkered under the desk. The figure looked just like his former girlfriend, Sally. When she got cross, sparks jumped from her hair. She had wanted Mike to join her at the University of York. On coming to college in London, he had lost contact with her.

The therapist's hand groped along the wall until she had a door handle in her fingers. She opened the door and jumped through into a shower room. She dived across the room and slammed her hands against the taps. Water spouted out as protection from the fire elemental.

Howling with a wonderful rage that enhanced her beauty, Smoky Sally turned back to the room. She billowed towards Mike.

He wanted to fling her to the floor. He needed her ripping away his clothes to meet with his urgent need. He crawled out from under the table to go to her without bothering to stand up.

Then Mr. Trewithick grabbed him and slapped him around the face, dragging him away.

'Apparently, I was wrong about you,' he shouted. 'Get out. It's a fire demon and a succubus.' He flung Mike at the door.

Mike skidded across the polished hardwood. Mr. Trewithick stood in the demon's path, holding it back to cover Mike's retreat.

He lifted a hand and shouted, '*Behold what was shaped in wickedness, but thou delightest not in burnt offerings.*'

Lightning crackled around the room.

Mr. Dunkley held his mirror in the air, catching each lightning strike that came off the creature and grounded it safely.

Mike remembered from his lessons that reflecting surfaces attracted lightning.

Around Dunkley the wooden floor smelled scorched. Mike could see that he kept his eyes away from unearthly beauty before him.

The creature backed away from Trewithick. The lightning hair flickered uncertainly. The clouds making up its form began to roil; with each word that hit it, more smoke drifted away.

Mike saw Sally fading away. 'No, don't leave me,' he whispered, lifting his hand to plead.

That simple belief was enough. The smoky figure reformed. A ball of lightning rolled from the creature's hand, hitting Trewithick in the chest.

He dropped to the floor.

The creature reached for Mike.

He needed Sally. He needed the feel of her hands on him, the taste of her in his mouth. He would take her here. Like last time when Sally had pulled him into the room in her hall of residence and locked the door. She had dragged his clothes off and...

'No!' Mike turned his head. 'No! That isn't what happened.'

He remembered the last time he had seen her, when he had thought it was forever. He could feel her lips against his, that clumsy first love.

Mr. Dunkley took a reluctant step to the center of the room.

'Take Trewithick,' he shouted.

Looking away from the creature that stalked men to their doom, Mike grabbed the shoulder of his fallen teacher and tugged him to the door.

Mr. Dunkley crouched and pulled a dirk from a sheath in his sock. He slipped the dirk into his pocket, calling out,

'He shall pour down rain upon sinners; fire and brimstone, storm and tempest shall be their portion to drink.'

His voice quavered in a way Mike had never heard before. He wondered whom Mr. Dunkley was seeing in the smoke. Never had Mike seen even him break into a sweat, but now he fell to his knees before this demon. His hand reached into his pocket and clenched.

As he pulled out the hand, Mike saw it was bleeding.

Dunkley knelt with his head bowed.

Mike had to distract the demon from its attack on Dunkley, to give the man more chance to recover.

A red LED light flickered in the corner of the room. Mike saw one of the air quality monitors. Skittering across the room, he shoved it into the smoky demon.

Smoke coiled towards the air intake grill. Strands of lightning flickered almost like ropes trying to latch onto something as the creature was sucked inside.

Sparks flared around the machine. They arced down the electrical wire. Mike yanked the cord out of the socket, isolating the creature in the machine.

Looking up, Dunkley saw what Mike had done. Wincing as he used his cut hand, he opened the filter housing and lifted out the charcoal filter. Smoke dripped to the floor, attempting escape.

'Quick,' he said, resting the filter on his mirror. 'Get a water bottle or a bowl or something.'

That made sense, water against a fire demon. Mike looked for a container. He found a flower vase. He pulled out the flowers and dumped them into the bin.

'Empty out the water,' Dunkley said.

Mike could see him sweating as if he'd been in a practice bout with swords against Mr. Trewithick. He whispered more words to keep the fire demon trapped.

It made no sense at all to Mike, water against fire surely. But he did as he was told and tipped the water out into a sink.

Dunkley crumbled the filter into the vase. He pulled a flask from his pocket. Mike knew that Mr. Dunkley's hip flask contained whisky, not brandy like Trewithick's. With a sour look on his face, he tipped the contents into the vase and swirled it.

'Bring me that funnel and a bit of cloth,' he said.

Mike did exactly as he was told, though by now he was far beyond his lessons in demon containment. Why hadn't Mr. Dunkley just put the filter into the water? Why all the games with the whisky?

'It seems Trewithick was right about you,' said Dunkley. He sounded disapproving.

'I'm not sure what you mean,' said Mike, cautiously.

'That you are not innocent,' said Dunkley.

Mike flushed. 'Only once,' he muttered.

'Remember,' Dunkley's voice was stronger now, 'that if you complete your training, your Oath of Office states that you will not put one person's needs first.'

'I know,' Mike sighed. 'Anyway, she dumped me. After I came to London she never wrote.'

Dunkley lifted an eyebrow, and then frowned. 'And while we are on the subject it's impolite to laugh at another's misfortunes.'

'What? Oh! The *Man Up*, sorry sir. Where I come from that phrase means stop whining.'

'Ah!'

Mike thought he saw a hint of humor in Dunkley's eyes as he flicked a glance at where Trewithick sprawled in the doorway.

Trewithick muttered something crude and sat up holding his head. Dunkley filtered the whisky back into his flask.

'You should have grabbed my flask,' Trewithick said.

'No time,' Dunkley said. 'Mine has a higher percent ABV anyway.'

Mike slipped over to the doorway to check on Mr. Trewithick.

'What's he doing? Why whisky?' Mike whispered to Mr. Trewithick.

'Firewater,' Mr. Trewithick said. He rubbed his temples as he spoke. 'It's high alcohol by volume for the spirit to infest. All we do now is pour it into a vat of blended whisky the next time Dunkley goes home. And we spread the demon among so many bottles that it will be impotent to attack anyone. The blended whisky from the Dunkley Estate is famous for its quality.'

'Why not just water? To put out the fire.'

'It was too powerful for that,' Mr. Trewithick said. 'Once a fire elemental manifests as plasma, well… You know how we're always told never to put water on an electrical fire? It's the same with elementals.'

The water in the shower room switched off. Dunkley and Trewithick heard it.

'She's not going to be happy that we're taking away her source of income,' Trewithick said.

With one thought, both men grabbed Mike and ran to the door—no one needed another fight today.

A scream of rage followed them downstairs.

The receptionist still sat on the floor looking blank.

Oh God! Mike thought, *that could have been me.* Just breathing the air in the gym was stifling. He outpaced his tutors and stood outside to stare at the blue, clear sky. It stopped him from thinking about the creature that had shown itself as Sally.

'All right there, Mike?' Trewithick asked.

Mr. Dunkley had moved to one side, glowering at some trees in the distance.

'That was an … um… odd experience,' Mike said. 'Cold shower time for me, I think.'

Trewithick snorted.

'Now that's over,' Mike said. 'At least all that's left is to tip the flask into a vat of blended.'

Mr. Trewithick made shushing motions at Mike with his hands.

Mr. Dunkley spun around. His eyes flared—Mike had never seen him angry before, only wry or resigned.

'This was Finest Single Malt from Islay. It's Caol Ila. To have to pour that pure grain spirit into a vat of blended…'

Trewithick patted Dunkley on the shoulder. 'Time to go and have a cold shower for you too, hey?'

Dunkley closed his eyes and clenched his fists. He took a deep, calming breath and opened them again. He turned on his heel and stalked to his car.

Mike mimed wiping sweat from his forehead as Dunkley drove away. 'And who does he see in a succubus?'

'Strange you should ask that. We both see someone we have loved, and can eventually forgive ourselves the …ah … strong feelings we experience.' Trewithick stared after Dunkley. 'Dunkley only sees the demon.'

Dancing Through the Night with You

'Move aside little third year, I want the news on.'

Mike looked up and scowled. He saw a tall man with black hair and blue eyes and relaxed a little.

'Oh come on, Dave,' Mike said. 'It's only ten minutes to the end of the footy.'

'I need the news now.'

Dave grabbed the remote from Mike. The television was a new innovation in the Students' Common Room. Unfortunately under College etiquette, fifth years had the right to precedence.

The room filled with the heartbeat top of the hour music on the 24-hour news channel.

Police investigating the odd case of the Dancing Pensioners at a Home near Romney Marsh in Kent...

'She got very confused just before she died,' the nurse said. 'She complained bitterly about the memory foam mattress—we put them on all the beds to reduce bedsores, you know. She kept going on about feather beds needing to be plumped up every day or else the devil could get your shape from the sleeper's imprint; it was what she was taught when she was a housemaid in a big house. She was so proud of having been *in service* when she was fourteen. But we said, "it's not a feather bed." But she never would understand. She refused to get out of bed the next day. Matron had her out in a flash, of course.'

Dave leaned on the wall next to her, trying to find a bit of shade out of the baking sun. 'I never heard that superstition before.' He looked at her name badge. 'Do you mind if I call you Jessica?'

'Okay then…She was old. They go funny towards the end and remember things from when they were girls. Why one of our dears keeps going on about fairy lights, and that started in May so why she was talking about Christmas I don't know.'

'Was she another one who did this *dancing* thing?'

Jessica blinked, then she smiled. 'Why yes, you are clever. Mrs. Carson was one the Dancers. You know, I wonder sometimes if the dancing is caused by marsh gas. The air gets all creepy and cold. And there's a dreadful mist crawls in off the marsh. I hate working on the nights like that. Putting the nursing home this close to the marsh was a really bad thing.'

'That's an interesting idea,' said Dave.

'I read, I think it was in school, that Romney Marsh was described as evil.'

Dave smirked. 'Ingoldsby, he wrote, "Grievous in winter, evil in summer and never good".'

'You're quite the scholar, aren't you?' said Jessica, leaning into him. 'Perhaps we could go somewhere after my shift and… discuss literature.'

Dave screwed up his face in disgust. He lifted his hand and said, '*Hide me from the gathering together of the froward.*' He paused as her face went blank. Then she blinked and shook her head.

'What were we talking about?' she said.

'You said you thought the dancing was caused by marsh gas, may I ask why?'

'Well, I used to work in a hospital, you know,' said Jessica. 'It was in London. We got patients in whose blood tests gave results like the ones we're getting here.'

'How?'

'The CK in the blood tests, creatine kinase,' said Jessica. 'It's a test for heart attacks—it tells you if any muscles have been damaged. Well, the blood tests I'm talking about had CKs something like ten times higher than in a heart attack, and they were all ecstasy users. So I figure the old dears have been given a drug. Matron monitors all drugs here, so it has to be an external influence. Which is why I thought of the marsh gas.'

Jessica turned and frowned at the trees that lay behind the fence of the nursing home grounds. A man who looked like he should be an inmate at the nursing home, not an employee, was mowing grass that looked like it needed watering not cutting.

Through the heat haze, Dave saw Mr. Dunkley walking towards him, those two brutes of dogs, Ross and Rory, panted at his heels.

'Thanks for the info, Jessica,' he said. 'That's my boss. I've got to go.'

'Oh! Right!'

Dave watched as Jessica appraised Mr. Dunkley. She straightened and stuck out her chest. It was just as well he had turned down her advances, if she had so little discernment as all that.

'David,' Dunkley's voice bore a trace of a Scots accent. 'Have you finished here?'

'Yeah, see you, Jessica.'

As they walked away, Dunkley spoke. 'And now what do you think should be done?'

'She thinks it's in the marsh, so I'd like to work on an idea of mine.' Dave looked slyly at Dunkley.

Dunkley stepped away and spread his hands, in a-go-for-it expression.

Dave licked his lips nervously. 'I need to be on the spot where the dancing took place. The police report says that we can access this part of the marsh from a gate in the lane.'

Dunkley gestured him to lead the way.

The thought of those two hounds behind him had Dave waking briskly away.

As they passed Dunkley's people carrier, Dunkley said, 'Take it from here, then David.' He opened his car door and leaned in for a thermos flask.

'What me?' said Dave. 'On my own?'

'You've been studying at University for five years now—see what you can do.'

Dave heard the chink of ice cubes as Dunkley poured a drunk and settled into the passenger side. Ross sat begging for biscuits; Rory lay in the shade waiting.

For a moment, Dave stood frozen. Then he spun around and opened the gate into the marsh. He was really getting to do something on his own. He knew the other two fifth years and one of the fourth years had been working solo, but finally Dunkley was letting him off the lead. The tutor may have been good at training dogs but at training witch finders he was lousy.

Dave had been ready for this moment for months.

But first. *'From the Ungodly shall Thy acts be hidden.'* That should stop Dunkley, or anyone, from stealing his ideas.

As he reached the marshy ground he recited, *'Who divided the Red Sea...'* He stopped before he reached the end of the incantation. No, he wasn't going to do it that way. What he knew, what none of the other lazy sods at college knew, was that the mnemonics from Common Prayer that Dunkley put in his workings were unnecessary. The poetry of Common Prayer was simply something people could remember it in a hurry. They heard it every Sunday in chapel—if they stayed awake.

'Give me dry feet,' he said. He stepped out, letting the working spread into the marsh. *And lo*, Dave thought, *my feet are dry.*

He followed a series of stakes that the police had left, as a trail through the marsh, each linked to the next with that yellow and black police warning tape held out of the mud by iron spikes. The line led to a piece of high ground—well it was a large hummock—also taped off. Even without the police markings, the ring of toadstools that grew around the edges would have attracted his attention to the dancing ring.

In a way it was lucky that the old dear had died during her dance. They'd never have been called in, if the old folk had just continued dancing, until the demon grew too powerful to contain.

Lifting up the tape he slipped under and stood, just breathing. He let his breathing deepen and felt for his heartbeat, slow and steady, despite his excitement. Finally, he was being allowed to follow an investigation through to the end. He found his center, as easily as if he were in the training classrooms at college, and began to work—silently.

His working spread through the layers of the swamp. Wheedling, cajoling, coaxing the past, he gradually brought into focus images of the people who had been here.

The old lady walked blindly through the trees and marsh grass, eyes open but seeing nothing but the firefly light that led her on. She was barefoot, and the hem of her pink, nylon nightie dragged in the mud.

Marsh gas indeed, thought Dave. *That's how most people explain away Will o'the Wisp stories these days.*

And a human, a man stood waiting for her.

Witch-Finder

The cast of characters came visible to his backward seeing eyes.

'Come to me.' He broke his silence and whispered into the breeze, which stroked through the leaves and bent the grass stalks. *'From the depths I call to you.'*

Now all I have to do is wait, thought Dave. Those responsible will arrive here and I can turn them over to the police.

He had always felt that the fighting the Witch Finder College taught was an unnecessary overhang from the old, unenlightened days. He could feel his working gently spreading like an incoming tide, along the trail of the old woman back to the nursing home. He felt it connect.

Dave sat on a fallen tree trunk. He pulled his jacket closed. He was getting cold sitting here out of the sun. It was odd the way the trees blocked out most of the sun, so although the heat on the lawn was stifling it was quite chill in here. Still, it was bright, even though the mist of the previous night clung to the roots and in the shade of the trees.

Coming up from the Nursing Home, on the path the pensioners had been led Dave saw a figure, being compelled, just like his victims. *Justice really*, Dave thought.

The groundsman emerged from the shadows. He carried an old style gas lantern.

'Now, put aside your lamp, and let's go to the police station.' Dave smirked at the elderly man. This way had been so easy. Now everyone would have to listen when he explained how wrong the old ways were.

The man reached up to his lantern and flicked open the hatch. Mist hissed out, lighted from within. The mist swirled around Dave.

He scrambled to his feet but it was too late. The flickering fairylight from the mist was in his face, and Dave breathed it in

He jerked legs and arms working like a robot. He tried coughing; he had to get the Wisp out of his system. Gasping, he tried to remember what he had worked out for exorcism. But he could only cough, like he had a crumb stuck in his windpipe.

'C-c-c-a-st.' He failed even to stammer out the old prayers that Dunkley used.

The groundsman smiled, a broad grin that showed off his nicotine yellow teeth. He lifted a hand.

'Dance for me then,' he said. He held out a cigarette lighter. 'You know what I do to creatures that don't dance.'

The creature inside Dave flinched away from the naked flame.

The groundsman stepped closer.

Dave's eyes locked onto the flame with which the groundsman tormented the water elemental inside him.

'I have to work, while they lounge about in luxury,' the groundsman said. *'Their* pensions weren't stolen by the government.'

Dave's feet shuffled, then began to prance. His arms fluttered about doing a disco jive to some music heard only by the old man. He coughed again, still trying to dislodge the creature from his lungs.

He had lost his breath and his voice as his head began to roll about in neck spraining twirls.

The groundsman stepped forward again flicking on the lighter.

'Come on my little fairy, dance for Daddy.'

'Not easy, Daddy,' whispered Dave's voice. 'Not without knowing his shape. Let me out, Daddy. It hurts.'

The only answer the Wisp got was the lighter moving closer.

Where was Dunkley? He should have been running to his apprentice's aid as he always had before. Then Dave remembered the blocking spell he had worked just before entering the marsh. Dunkley would never know he was in danger. His heart pounded—he couldn't break free.

He shared the fear of the Wisp in his body.

It upped the pace.

Dave felt his body twist and twirl, then lunge and spring. The creature made his body do stag jumps, forcing unpracticed muscles to complain.

While the Wisp concentrated on making the jumps Dave worked on getting his mouth free.

'*Deliver me from the hand of mine enemies,*' he gasped.

The Wisp bit his tongue. He tasted blood as it trickled down his throat. Then he began an intricate hand jive.

'That's right, little fairy.' The groundsman waved his lighter in time to whatever music he heard.

Dunkley charged into the clearing. 'ROSS! *Ceart.*'

The dog moved away to the right to tackle the man while Rory stayed at heel.

'The wicked man will take little fairy from Daddy. Kill him fairy.' The groundsman waved his lighter at Ross, who growled and stalked him low to the ground. The wolfhounds were not that far removed from wolves. The man lashed out with the hand that held the lighter. It singed the fur over Ross's ear.

'ROSS!' shouted Dunkley. '*Gluas air falbh.*' The dog backed off.

Dave's body moved, still under control of the elemental. He yanked out one of the iron spikes that held the police tape and charged at Dunkley.

If the spirit killed Dunkley, Dave knew he'd be helpless. He struggled with the Wisp inside him. As he'd hoped, the creature didn't have full control over his body. The pair of them fought over control for his muscles. Dave made it lurch as it struck at Dunkley.

At where Dunkley had been. The man moved like the wind.

'Rory, *cum air ais a,*' said Dunkley, in low voice.

Rory growled at Dave. The huge dog crouched, ready to attack.

Dave seized control of his legs and backed up. The dog's growling eased but he stood between Dave and where Dunkley stood, trying to reach the groundsman.

As the threat from the dog subsided, the Wisp fought Dave's control. The iron pole swung round, the body tottered, neither of them in charge.

They staggered about in the body they shared until they tripped over a log.

56

Dave's body fell heavily over Rory.

Something crunched. The dog lay still under them.

'Fairy, help me,' shouted the groundsman.

The head swung toward the spirit's *Daddy.*

The old groundsman moved stiffly, as he tried to dodge Dunkley.

Dave desperately tried to get his head to swing around. He had to see the damage to Rory.

The Wisp got a grip on Dave's body again. It clenched the iron pole and charged with the spike towards Dunkley. The witch finder whisked out of the way, but Daddy was too slow. The spike speared his throat, severing the artery. Blood spurted, mixing with the mud and the marsh grass.

A keening wail sounded from between Dave's lips as the Wisp realized what it had done.

'Cast out sin, the devil and all his works,' Dunkley shouted.

Dave felt the working coursing through his blood like fire, burning out the poison of the infestation. He felt as if a hook was clamped into his lungs pulling them inside out, and out of his throat.

With a great whooping cough, light jetted out of his mouth and nose. The Wisp darted away into the trees.

'You idiot!' Dunkley swung to face Dave. 'What the hell did you think you were doing blocking out your back-up like that. I thought you would do a simple divination. What possessed you to summon the culprit and his Wisp to you?'

Dave fell to the ground gasping for breath. He felt like someone had run him over with a steamroller or had stretched him on the rack. Dunkley grabbed the front of his shirt and hoisted him to his feet.

'Answer me!' shouted Dunkley.

Behind Dunkley, Dave saw Ross nuzzling at Rory, who sprawled unable to move. Ross sat back and howled, in a long aching note, not far from the call of a wolf.

Dunkley followed his student's gaze. He flung Dave away. Dave tripped over the police tape as he staggered away and landed hard on his backside.

'Rory.' Dunkley knelt over his fallen dog.

Rory whimpered.

With one hand on the dog's head Dunkley whispered, 'Go back to the car, David.'

Dave swallowed. Using a tree he managed to get to his feet. He thought that the angle of the dog's back was totally unnatural. He saw Dunkley reach for the dirk he wore in a sock sheath.

Behind them in the marsh, a fairylight flickered.

'Mr. Dunkley…'

'I said get going…' Dunkley hissed.

Dave fled. He barely noticed where his feet touched, but by the time he was on the road, his shoes were soaked through. Leaning on the people carrier he gasped for breath, trying to force down his fear and his tears for the dog.

He had managed to get one of Mr. Dunkley's precious wolfhounds killed.

The car was locked so Dave slid down the side and sat on the grass. He bowed his head into his arms and waited.

Around him in the lane the afternoon light faded. Over in the Nursing Home the lights came on and the nurses pulled the curtains across the windows to shut out the dangers of the night. Just along the lane a street lamp flared red, and gradually warmed into orange.

A noise sounded in the bushes nearby. A marble-faced Dunkley walked out. At his feet frolicked … two wolfhounds.

'Rory's OK,' whispered Dave.

Dunkley shrugged. 'He was a little stunned that's all.'

Dave looked at the dogs, neither of them had any marks of the fight on them. Even the burn over Ross's ear was gone. Dave watched Dunkley slide open the back door on the people carrier.

'*Thugainn thu*,' he said, calling to the dogs. They jumped in and, obedient as always, they went straight to their harnesses. Rory looked up at Dave, there was a glint of a firefly light in his eye.

It was just a reflection from the streetlights, Dave thought. What else could it be? Healing must be part of the course that Dave hadn't reached yet.

… have said that they are no longer looking for anyone in connection with the case after finding the body of the groundsman in his shed.'

Mike looked over at Dave. The man was white. His eyes were fixed on the door.

Mr. Dunkley, Dave's tutor, stood in the doorway, looking grave.

He paced across the room and handed Dave a brown envelope.

With shaking hands Dave ripped it open.

He pulled out a simple slip. He stared at it in disbelief for a moment, then anger suffused his face. Rising up like a volcano, he stood, nose to nose with Dunkley.

Mike tensed, prepared to intervene. He knew someone who would not want Dave hurt.

'I'd have passed if I'd had a better tutor,' Dave shouted.

'We were matched,' Dunkley said. 'Because the council felt that you would make a good theoretician. You would, I agree, but you have to be at least competent in the field or you fail.'

'I saw what you did,' Dave hissed. 'Is that why I've failed?'

'What do you think you saw?' Dunkley sneered. 'If I had a secret I wanted to keep, I would have advised the council to pass you, don't you think?'

After a hanging moment, Dave crumpled the slip and flung it at the bin. He brushed roughly past Mr. Dunkley and stalked out of the room.

Mr. Dunkley looked gravely at the remaining two fifth years present.

Casting glances at the other two, Mike walked across the room to the bin. He picked up the crumpled note, and smoothed out the paper.

Witch-Finder

The Council regrets to inform Mr. David Green that he has failed his fifth year examination.

Mike looked up at Mr. Dunkley.

'What happens now, sir?'

'Everyone who fails the year five exams leaves,' Dunkley said. 'Don't worry too much about him, Michael. He knew he would not qualify for his License to Practice. Why else would he have married your sister, against all the Oaths of Office we have to take?'

Mike swallowed. 'You know about that?'

Mr. Dunkley nodded. He left the Student's Common Room.

Say it with Flowers

We love you. Stay with us, be compost for us.

Penny whipped her head around, looking for the source of the noise.

She switched the cleaver to her left hand. Reaching into her coat pocket she pulled out a torch and flicked it on. The light glinted off grass heads turned into filigree ice statues by the hoarfrost. Here in the lane the air was still; her smoky breath hung in the air. Overhead the night breeze hushed through the tallest trees.

An iron gate barred the way through the hedge; it should have been chained and padlocked, but these lay on the path. Over the November just past, people had talked about lights that drifted through the garden center late at night.

She gripped the cleaver more tightly in her left hand—perhaps she should go back and leave the let's-play-at-witches to find out for themselves what, or rather who, was coming.

Sometimes, Penny felt they knew nothing of the game they played. The quarter moon hung in a cloudless sky—nothing occult would be happening; occult required the dark or the full moon, the bit in between was insignificant. Or so the other girls at school believed.

She remembered the gossip in the common room she'd overheard. Well okay, she had been hiding behind a curtain while the fools had discussed their next game.

'We'll get into awful trouble,' Chloë said. Penny had imagined her eyes gleaming with anticipation. 'You know Miss Hutton will confine us to school if she finds out we left the grounds after dark.'

'It's such a good place to do our ritual,' Mandy said.

Another girl that Penny hadn't known immediately chipped in, 'And if we are caught there, it does belong to my Dad.' Then Penny had recognized Lucy, who lived near-by but was a weekly-boarder to participate in evening activities.

Penny sighed. She had played occult games to the death, well not hers obviously, but her father and aunt were dead—killed by their belief—and her mother was still in prison for deliberately putting her son, Penny's older half-brother Karl, in danger.

Personally, Penny believed in the cleaver.

It was the other conversation that she had *overheard* that had her at the garden center in Whitton on Marsh after lights out. The one the head teacher, Miss Hutton, had with Mr. Dunkley. He wasn't a teacher at school—he had sorted out the mess the last time Penny had gone head on with the occult.

She hefted her cleaver and realized that her hand was shaking. There was a phone in her pocket—if it all went wrong she could still phone Mr. Dunkley.

She crept to the iron gate. She heard nothing.

She eased the latch.

It swung invitingly open.

It offended her that the iron gate opened noiselessly. It ought to let out a blood-curdling screech.

Penny ran her torch over the concrete slabs that cut a straight path through the display garden to the main entrance. The Christmas lights display, draped over the front of the building, glowed in a strident welcome.

Still there was no noise. No cats crept through the undergrowth to catch birds that made no sleepy twitterings. Jack Frost ran his fingers down her back.

She lifted the light from the path and studied the garden.

It was deliberately wild, in keeping with the current fashion. The gardener at her guardian's house would have resigned over fruit trees, in dire need of a pruning, growing to the left of the gate. In the upper branches of one she saw a twiggy mass.

She peered into the darkness—the tree was too low to attract an untidy rooks' nest and too big to belong to another bird.

Her stomach quivered at the thought of those massive untamed shrubs stroking her hair. So she continued walking up the path.

Hollyhocks and foxgloves grew tall in the path borders. Her coat brushed against rosemary and lavender lifting the scent to her nose. Global warming was interfering with the growing seasons, but this was the first of December, those plants should be long finished.

Her feet tapped a light rhythm on the path.

'Jack? Is that you?'

Penny recognized Mr. Dunkley's voice. She turned back to the gate, expecting to see Mr. Dunkley striding along the path, but there was no one. He must be in the garden already. Damn! He'd got here first.

She had hoped that Miss Hutton would keep him talking longer than that. She peered into the enveloping dark of the undergrowth, but no was visible.

'Mr. Dunkley? It's Penny Bailey, we met at Patrick Brompton two years ago.'

'Patrick Brompton? Oh yes! Yorkshire. I remember. Do not move off the path.'

'I'm standing still.' She felt like an ice statue in the moonlight.

'Now,' said Dunkley. 'Do you have a knife on you?'

'Umm… I've got a cleaver, will that do?' She hefted the borrowed weapon.

'You're better prepared this time,' he said. 'I shouldn't ask you to do this, but I'm trapped. I need you to do exactly as I say. Cut at every piece of vegetation in your path. Chop everything. Let nothing touch you.'

Penny peered into the gloom, waving her torch over where she thought his voice was coming from. 'Where are you?'

In the light she saw some petals drifting from a wild eglantine as the branches thrashed.

'Inside this rose bush and waiting for my back up, who is late.' There was an edge to Dunkley's voice now. 'Even if the plant looks harmless chop it.'

Penny switched the torch to her left hand. With the cleaver in her right, she swiped at a lavender bush in the border in front of her. The flower heads pulled away. Penny jumped back. 'They're alive.'

'What do they teach in Biology these days?' said Mr. Dunkley. He sounded strained, his accent lost most of the southern English and jumped straight back to Scottish.

Penny flushed. 'Well of course they are alive, but what I mean is… Oh heck.'

She hacked at the plant and then the next. She stomped on the grass that tried to spike her ankles. She stood in front of a wild rose bush. She could just make out a slouched form wrapped in rose thorns.

'That's it,' Dunkley said from inside. 'Toss that cleaver in here. And run back to the path.'

'What?' Penny looked at the leaf-stained, sharp edge of the cleaver. 'Throw it at you?'

'Look, just do it.' Dunkley's voice was little more than a gasp. 'There's no time to argue. Hard as you can, now.'

Penny hurled the heavy blade. Her rational mind said it must have been the wind that caused the rose branches to sway around as if they were trying to grasp and block the cleaver from getting to Mr. Dunkley. Then she stomped at the grass under foot that had taken advantage of her distraction to start needling at her ankles again.

Holly branches, which stood next to the roses, reached out for her. The red berries looked black like old blood in half-lit moonlight.

She backed away then fled through her cleared jungle path to the concrete slabs. The plants started reaching for her the moment that she neared them without hacking. They seemed to know she no longer had protection.

Panting, she stood in the middle of the path as far as possible from the lashing plants trying to reach her from the border.

Two huge dogs lunged out of the undergrowth and whimpered at her ankles, trying to hide behind her.

She felt dizzy as she hunkered down to reassure them and ended up sat on the cool slab burying her face in the nearest dog. The other licked at her hand. She could feel the rough tongue. It was so like Mr. Dunkley to free his dogs first, but when was he going to get here?

Mr. Dunkley burst through the hollyhocks brandishing the cleaver. Towering giants that would have won prizes at the Chelsea Flower Show fell to his vicious hacking. The wild garden had pulled wispy stands of his hair free of his waist-length plait. He stood for a moment, panting hard, and then he crouched next to her.

'Someone or ones have made a right mess here. Thanks for your help, Penny.' He sagged as one of his dogs started to lick his face, then ran a tired hand over the wiry fur on its back before moving on to the one Penny was hugging. 'Well they're fine. I need to grow a pelt like theirs to protect me.'

'Are you all right?' Penny asked. She flicked up her torch without shining it directly into his eyes. His face and hands looked red and bruised, covered in scratches that were beginning to swell up, as if he had an allergic reaction to rose thorns

'I've felt better. Let's get you out of here. Whoever is in that building is alerted to my presence by now, anyway.'

It was an effort for him to get to his feet. Finally standing, he waited to catch his breath. Penny tucked her shoulder under his arm, feeling worried.

'What happened?'

'The roses decided to turn me into compost by sucking me dry,' he said. At Penny's blank look he added, 'of blood.'

'Vampire Plants!' she said. 'Normal roses are bad enough, they don't need to be blood-suckers too.'

The dogs slunk up to him almost tripping them both. One of them gruffed, holding the two people back.

Dunkley gripped tight on her shoulder.

'What?' asked Penny. She wanted to be out of here

'I'm used to trusting my dogs' senses above mine,' he said.

He lifted his arm off her supporting shoulder and took a hesitant step toward the gate.

The plants in the borders lashed at them.

Dunkley shoved Penny into the safety of the wooden gazebo that the garden center employees had made into a porch over the main entrance.

Every part of the display garden was now a complete wall of plants locking them in—even the water lilies in the fishpond were snapping white petals. He turned to Penny. 'While I'm grateful for your help, why are you here?'

She shrugged. 'I wanted to warn the let's-play-at-witches that you were on your way. I didn't want them to get into trouble.'

'Are they friends of yours?'

Penny shook her head. 'Not close friends, but well, you're a witch finder.'

'We hardly ever burn witches at the stake these days. I think it might be against the rules,' he said dryly. He checked his watch. 'I have back-up on the way. Admittedly, he should have been here half an hour ago, but what support had you available?'

'I had my mobile with me,' said Penny. 'If it got too much I was going to call you.'

'Ah! A mobile phone, great help when movement causes attack,' he said.

Something stroked her leg. Penny screamed and pressed against the glass door, where the garden center employees had hung a holly and mistletoe wreath. A Gardenia plant in a pot reached with hairy leaves, looking for a way past Penny's protective jeans. Weakly, Dunkley knocked it over. Penny kicked it; the pot plant flew out into the garden where some azaleas clawed at it, shredding the succulent's leaves.

'If I might?' Dunkley gestured to Penny's torch.

She handed it over and he checked out the door. 'It looks like someone has wedged this closed. Hmmm.' He returned the light to Penny. 'Let's see if we can get in.'

He wrapped his sleeve over the fist clenched around the torch and punched through the glass window of the door. The safety glass shattered into small cubes, which tinkled to the ground.

He reached in, shoving hard on something then pushed on the door to slide it sideways.

'Won't they prosecute you?' said Penny. 'That's break and entry.'

'People generally don't.' Finally the door gave a little. He sniffed at the air. So did the dogs, they growled a low note. 'Perhaps you should wait here.'

'With all these man-eating plants?' she said.

'You have a point.' He slipped inside, motioning his dogs to stay between Penny and the garden. She heard the sound of wheels squealing then the door opened far enough that she and the dogs could get in.

Looking around, by the light of the torch, she realized that there had been a heavy-duty trolley barring the door.

'They barricaded themselves in,' she said.

'Looks like.' He prowled into the hall. 'Now stay here, please Penny. There might be things you shouldn't see.'

'Worse than seeing my dad blown to bits by lightning?' she said.

'Probably not, but perhaps we should limit your exposure to nastiness,' he said. 'I think that you won't even be sixteen, yet.'

Penny shrugged and followed him up the ramp into the main center. She ran her torchlight over the displays near the checkout. There were shirts embroidered with owls and indoor plants crowding the space with *Christmas Presents for Her*—all-natural cosmetics—piled on the wall shelves.

'Ah!' Dunkley strode to one side. 'That's what I need.'

Penny watched him make for a fridge unit, glowing with internal light. With a quick glance around the huge shed, he opened the fridge and took out a bottle of water. He gulped it down and reached for a second.

Penny stared at him.

'I'm a bit dehydrated,' he said. 'Having your blood sucked out by vampire plants tends to do that.'

The warehouse was more than just a garden center. To one side she saw a poster for flat roof repair. Her torchlight glinted off the glass in the models that advertised the conservatory builders. On the other side of the artificial and real Christmas trees, which stood around looking pretty, a company fitting Agas and wood-burning stoves had set up home. The trees rustled.

'They're in here too, Mr. Dunkley.' Penny stepped back.

Dunkley dropped the water bottle into his pocket. 'Ross, *ceart*. Rory, *cearr*.'

The two dogs split and circled right and left towards the trees.

'Penny?' said a voice. Hands parted the trees and a girl stepped out. 'Penny Bailey? Have you brought someone to rescue us?' She blinked in the light of the torch shining on her.

'That's Lucy,' said Penny. 'Her Dad owns this Garden Center.'

The three girls from school pushed their way out of the Christmas display. They all looked up at Dunkley.

Typical, Penny thought. *Look to the man to sort out the mess.*

Dunkley pulled out the water bottle and took another swig. 'So what happened here?'

Penny bit her tongue. She wanted to tell them to be careful of what they said.

Dunkley flicked a glance her way. He looked amused—as if he knew the struggle with her conscience.

'Just to put Penny at ease. I should tell you my name is Dunkley. I'm… well, it's easiest to think of me as a witch finder. So how did you create that mess out there?'

'We didn't do it,' Chloë said. 'It must have been the people here at the garden center.'

'I think Dad's people had a clear out of the stock room to make room for the Christmas decorations.'

Mandy joined in. 'We washed out the out-of-date fertilizer bottles and used them to store our Love Potion, but they're not there anymore.'

'We came up here tonight, because it's December first,' Lucy said. 'Chloë's book said it was a good date for scrying out which boys to use it on.'

Penny bit harder into her tongue, but it was no use—she sniggered.

Dunkley looked at her with his eyebrows raised.

'What's so funny?' Chloë demanded. 'We spent hours working out that formula. Then it all got dumped on the garden.'

Penny tried to stop laughing. 'It's ridiculous, such a waste of time. One of your hairs—to bind around his heart—in food or drink would work just as well.'

'And how would you know?' Chloë demanded.

Penny opened her mouth to answer.

'Actually, it's a severe misuse of Cræft,' Dunkley interrupted. 'Any coercion of another's will is a bad idea.' The torchlight glinting in his hazel eyes made him look like a mad prophet. The loose, wispy ends of his hair stood out, and sparked.

Penny stopped laughing. She licked her lips. The other girls huddled into a group.

Dunkley swigged from his bottle.

'You have created this mess,' he said, his face like marble. 'How do you intend to clear it up?'

'But we didn't,' Chloë said. 'We explained. It was the garden center staff.'

'When I tell my Dad,' Lucy said. 'I'm sure he'll understand.'

'*I* am the only authority who matters,' Dunkley said. He pulled up a chair from the garden furniture section and sat down with a sigh. '*Thugainn thu.*'

The two dogs slid away from the girls and came to sit on alert at his side.

'Can't you get us out?' Mandy asked.

'I can get myself and Penny out of here, at any point,' he said. 'I could even help you sort out this mess, but I don't feel like it right now.'

Chloë glared at Penny. 'What did you have to bring him here for?'

'She came on her own,' Dunkley said, 'to warn you of my imminent arrival. *I* read the diaries you left in your bedrooms at school.'

Three mouths dropped open in horror. Penny flicked a glance at Dunkley. She hoped he hadn't read her diary.

'But they're *private*!' protested Chloë. 'Miss Hutton wouldn't let you look in those.'

Dunkley shrugged. 'Think what you wish. Your safety was more on Miss Hutton's mind. Now how are you going to get out of here?'

They looked at each other. Lucy studied Mr. Dunkley, who was scratching one of his dogs' ears. She sidled over to Penny.

'How do you normally break a love spell, then?'

Penny thought for a moment then said, 'The usual way is to give the lover a knife. But I don't see how a plant could accept it.'

'Hey!' Mandy said, 'I've got a great idea. I saw them just back here.' She ploughed in between the Christmas trees.

'Penny,' Dunkley said, without looking up from his dogs. 'I would appreciate it if you would let the girls sort this out for themselves.'

'He's grumpy one, isn't he?' Lucy asked.

'I think I'd be a bit grumpy if I'd been attacked by blood-sucking roses out to turn me into compost,' Penny answered. She walked stiffly over to the table where Dunkley sat. 'They're never going to sort it out by themselves. Let me help.'

'They need to learn a lesson.'

Penny slumped into the chair opposite him.

Mandy emerged from the trees carrying a long box. 'Look! It's a flaming weed killer. You just add these butane bottles and we can burn plants out there.'

Lucy groaned. 'My Dad's going to kill me!'

Dunkley looked at the box then Mandy's eager face. 'What a good idea,' he said. 'I've always wanted to set something alight when I'm stuck in the middle of it.'

Mandy put down the box.

'This isn't getting me any friends here.' Penny shrunk further into her seat as Chloë and Mandy glared at Dunkley.

'Is being friends with them that important?' asked Dunkley.

'How old *are* you?'

'What I meant was, are there no other girls who share your interests more closely with whom you can be friends?'

'Yeah, guess so. But this lot can make life uncomfortable for me. A boarding school's a pretty closed system, you know.'

'Actually, I do,' said Dunkley. He smiled slightly. 'I remember decking Bryce, he was sixth form and I was first, because he wanted...' He cleared his throat. 'Anyway that was the bad old days. Perhaps you could help them. Go, if you really want to.'

Penny jumped to her feet. She trotted over to where the other girls were in a huddle.

'Are you sure you want to touch us, after your snooty friend says you're not to?' Chloë sniffed.

'Well, I would like to get out of here and back to school. I'm sleepy,' Penny said. 'And I think he might be inclined to keep you here until you're done.'

'Look,' Lucy said. 'It's clear that Penny knows a bit about this stuff, can we just ask her advice, please?'

'It's not our fault,' Mandy said. 'Why should we clean up the mess caused by their clear up?'

'You should never have made a love potion in the first place,' Penny explained. 'And in the second, you should have guarded it better.'

'Stop arguing,' Lucy said. 'Now Penny, how do we go about clearing up this problem?'

'I want to know Penny's credentials,' Chloë insisted.

'Shut up,' Lucy screamed. 'I don't care. We've got to stop those plants before my Dad opens the center in the morning.'

Chloë stomped off. 'Fine you listen to someone else. I've got books on this subject. I know what I'm talking about.'

Mandy looked between Lucy and Chloë.

Dunkley glanced up from his dogs. 'When people write Cræft down they usually skip important details. And for your information, Penny's father worked in Cræft. It got him killed. So she knows better than to get mixed up with dabblers like you, yet she still wanted to spare you an investigation of my office.'

Penny looked at the other girls. Chloë hovered at the edge, Penny could see she was in a grump about taking a lesser role than leadership.

'Chloë,' Penny said. 'What do your books say about removing a love curse? None of the remedies I know would work here—they are only for people.'

Chloë handed over her glossy covered book. 'Why are you asking me? *He* said that my books are useless.'

'But they are likely to have only a small bit removed, to make them safe,' said Penny. 'We should be able to work out what the missing part is, if we put our heads together.'

'It's not a *love curse* as you call it,' Chloë said. 'The recipe is for a love potion.'

Penny eyed Chloë. 'Anything that makes someone do something that they wouldn't normally do is a curse. Let's work on getting out through the plants and back to school, then we can decide what to do about the curse.'

'No!' Lucy wailed. 'My Dad'll kill me if people can't get into the Garden Center. I'll get taken away from school!'

'I think they will only come alive like this after dark,' said Penny. 'Is that right Mr. Dunkley?'

'Yes,' he said. 'The Cræft used here has attracted a water elemental, which has infested the garden. Sunlight, being a symbol of fire, will make the plants inert.'

Penny flicked to the index of Chloë's book. Out of curiosity she turned to *V*. There in black and white it said *vampire plants p64*. Unable to believe it, Penny turned to page sixty-four.

'Oh!' she said, disappointed. 'It's only about Mistletoe. I thought we had our answer for a moment there.'

'My Dad got the mistletoe for the center wreaths, and for the one on our house, from a tree here in the garden,' Lucy said.

Penny read on. According to the book some people thought that mistletoe was the spirit of the oak tree, because it was evergreen. She shut the book, there was no help for this problem there.

'How about pheromones?' Mandy asked. 'Can plants sense them? If we cover ourselves in the natural flower perfumes from that display over there, they might let us go through, because they won't sense the human pheromones.'

The girls looked at each other, but no one could think of a better idea.

'But I'm taking one of those flame weed killers too,' said Mandy. 'That way we can threaten the plants with flame if they attack us.'

The other girls dashed around and doused themselves with perfume. Penny checked on Dunkley. He had finished three bottles of water and looked a lot better. He stacked the bottles at the checkout and left the correct purchase price in coins on the desk.

Penny considered the much more expensive perfumes the girls had doused themselves in.

'Penny,' Dunkley strolled up to her. 'Stick close to me, please.'

'Isn't this going to get us past the frakenflowers?' she whispered.

'I've no idea,' he answered. 'Elementals believe what their worshippers believe, so it might work. But I'd like to be able to get you out of danger if anything happens, before I fish out these little brats.'

His dogs trotted at his heels.

Mandy grabbed one of the flame weed-killers. Chloë hugged her precious book. Then they walked out down the concrete path. The plants barely stirred in the wind.

Maybe, thought Penny, this mad idea is going to work.

Then Chloë tripped over her feet. Automatically she held out her hands to break the fall. Her book fell in among the ornamental thistles and she stuffed her hand in to retrieve it before Penny could stop her.

A thorn scraped the back of her hand.

Penny saw the blood well up, black in the half-light, then saw Chloë's head nodded forwards, sleepily.

'But we've doused ourselves in the essence of dead plants,' Lucy whispered.

The Hollyhocks brushed their leaves over their shoulders, tasting the essence of dead flowers.

'Don't listen to her,' shouted Penny. 'Believe it will work.'

The night breeze brought anticipatory rustlings from the plants: stay with us, we love you, be our compost.

Lavender heads speared at their legs.

'Get going!' Mandy shrieked. She pushed Chloë out of the way and fired her weed-killer into the border.

Blossoms of flame appeared on the ends of burning stalks. Bushes of rosemary and lavender frantically tried to thrash out their burning leaves.

'That's done it,' Dunkley said. 'Run!' He faced the garden center, turning his head, searching for something.

Penny heard footsteps sprinting down the path. She saw the fruit trees bending away from the fire. The huge mass in the upper branches swayed about dizzily to avoid the sparks. Then she realized what Dunkley was seeking, the elemental spirit that had infested the garden.

'It's in the Mistletoe,' she shouted at Dunkley, pointing to the mass in the apple tree.

Dunkley turned and muttered to himself as he lifted his hands. Between his fingers, tame lightning crackled. Just like she had heard St. Elmo's fire described.

Dunkley lifted his chin. His voice echoed oddly around the garden. '*And I listened to the Voice as a great Fire rushed through the bushes.*'

The bundle of mistletoe screamed as it burst into flames. The bushfire in the border had spread, setting light to other plants. Penny could see the leaves of the holly bush outlined against the flame that started inside it. It was beautiful.

'Penny,' Dunkley shouted.

Penny jerked out of her reverie and saw that he and the dogs were already halfway to the gate.

Chloë sat on the path dreamily staring at her precious book in the middle of the burning border.

Penny scrambled along the path. The heat was already intense. The wisteria that climbed up over the house was ablaze. The roof of the porch was smoking and starting to glow.

Chloë tried reaching her hand into the flames to get her book. Penny grabbed her by the collar and wrenched her up. She slapped Chloë's face.

'Get out of here, you idiot.'

Awakened from her plant-induced dream, Chloë lifted up her arms to cover her face and staggered through the burning torches, which used to be hollyhocks and foxgloves, lighting the path to the gate.

Following Chloë, Penny wondered if she was going to be burned alive. Her hair felt like it was melting in the heat. It was too hot to breathe. A simple breath set her coughing.

Suddenly, her wrist was grabbed. Strong hands dragged her through the burning plants. Through squinting eyes she could see the dark hedge looming up out of the bright, burning garden.

Cool air washed over her as she stumbled down the road away from the great conflagration.

'Oh no!' Lucy wailed. 'What's my Dad going to say?'

Opening her eyes, Penny discovered that she was lying on the grass next to Chloë. Sirens howled in the distance. Penny pushed up on one elbow and saw Mr. Dunkley walking away.

'Stop,' she said, jumping to her feet and running after him. Her raw face felt cooled by the icy breeze.

He turned to face her, with a quick glance to where the sirens were rapidly approaching.

'What are you going to do to them?' She waved a hand at the other girls.

'Me?' said Dunkley. 'I'll do nothing. My unwelcome presence in the neighborhood will not have gone unnoticed by the local practitioners. They and you, if you choose, will not go untaught for much longer.'

'I want to learn from you,' she said. 'I want to be a witch finder.'

'Impossible.'

'Why? Didn't I do good last time?'

'You left me very little to do,' he said.

'What about now? If I hadn't helped you'd still be stuck.'

'You were excellent as back-up.'

'So why can't I learn to be a witch finder?'

'For a start you're not eighteen, which is the minimum age for starting at our college.'

'Fine,' she said. 'I'll get there, but no doubt you have other excuses.'

'Of course.' His hazel eyes glinted in the firelight. 'It would cost too much money to change all the plumbing over to allow lady students.'

Lady students! Penny was speechless at this deliberate provocation.

He smiled at her and bowed slightly. He turned and called his dogs. He continued down the path, away from the approaching authorities, with the comfortable stride of someone who knows he has taken down another enemy.

Penny glared after him. No female witch finders, huh? She'd prove him wrong.

Long Shadows in the Night

Three of them stood looking at the drain under the streetlight.

Dunkley paced a few steps away, into the middle of the road and suspended his pendulum over the nearest access cover. The stark orange light made hideous shadow pictures across the road.

'Definitely down there,' he said. He wrapped the string of the pendulum into a neat ball and stowed it in the pocket of his trench coat. Thick clouds crowded in from the west, they seemed to fight each other for space as they reflected the orange glow of the town lights. It wasn't raining, yet.

Mike looked between the two older men, waiting to be told what would happen next.

Dunkley scratched his beard as he studied the drain. 'I think I'll get back to my Internet problem, if you don't mind,' he said to his colleague, Trewithick.

Trewithick was Mike's assigned tutor, though both older men worked so well as a team that they tended to go into the field together. He ignored Mike and looked at Dunkley with interest.

'Why have they called us in on something like that?'

'If you weren't such a Luddite I'd show you,' Dunkley said. 'A disconcerting number of people have died while sitting at the computer screen doing their Internet banking. I find coincidence is a difficult concept.'

'Ah! It's time I retired,' said Trewithick. He looked thoughtfully at his trainee, then back at the drain cover. 'Well Mike, how about you take it from here? I suppose I ought to understand this new threat.'

'What?' Mike glanced down at the sewer cover. 'I'm sure I'm not up to working alone.' He essayed a hopeful smile.

But Trewithick and Dunkley had turned away.

'Any pubs open in Barrow-in-Furness at two in the morning do you think?' Trewithick asked.

'I've got a thermos of tea in the car.' Dunkley turned back to see Mike hovering. 'Come to my car when you have some information for us.'

'See you in a bit, then,' Trewithick said.

Hopelessly, Mike crouched and used his hiking staff to lever up the access hatch. He took one last look after his tutors and sighed. Mr. Trewithick's blond hair was tied back in a ponytail, but Dunkley's brown plait swung like his pendulum. They seemed to be arguing about sugar. OK, so they had decided not to wade knee deep in the... well, he wasn't even going to think about it.

The dark hole lurked at his feet, a fetid odor whispered up from the depths. Open, it was a hazard for anyone walking late at night, but he felt unwilling to close the darkness over his head.

He touched his staff to the four cardinal points around the drain, saying, '*Let all those that seek thee, walk in safety.*'

He stripped off his good raincoat and laid it next to the opening. Looking down into the depths, he removed his watch and stuffed it in the coat pocket.

His mother had given him for his twenty-first, two years ago, and the air that drifted up from below felt corrosive enough to dull the shine.

Muttering an invocation against disease, and wishing he could think up something against the stink, he solidly placed his boots on the first rung of the ladder.

Breathing through his mouth, he flicked on the torch that hung from his belt—pointed down it let him see that this wasn't a deep drain. At the bottom he straddled the umm… liquid and unhooked his torch. He played the light over the Victorian brickwork of the tunnel. Ooze dripped from slime moulds growing on mortar.

Something scuttled. His heart leaped as he swung the torch. A tail vanished into the steam that rose off the sewage.

He caught his breath. He'd seen scarier things than rats in his training.

He turned the light on the tunnel the other way. Sitting on caterpillar treads was a robotic maintenance camera, daubed over with graffiti. Away from the ladder shaft, the roof was low. He bowed his lofty head and waddled along, trying to keep his feet dry.

Beyond the light of the torch he saw patches of phosphorescence joining in the dripping down the walls. He gathered his strength.

'*Open up mine eyes that I may see the wondrous things,*' he said.

Vapors swirled around his knees. Catching a future memory, he saw fire sweeping through the tunnel.

The motor on the robotic camera whirred into life, distracting him from seeing more. He blinked but the vision was gone.

Fire, he remembered that, but that was unlikely with all this liquid. He shrugged and set off after the robot, he wanted to examine the graffiti. After all, no self-respecting young vandal would come down here—no one would see his masterpiece.

Fire, the word nagged at him, but a fire elemental would not last down here with all the damp. *Fire damp*, thought Mike.

He heard something in the robot click.

His feet had started running to the entrance before he thought the word *methane*.

His heavy boots splashed through the liquid. He heaved himself onto the ladder and scrambled up the greasy rungs, his boots slipping in the slime. He crawled onto the road and pushed at the cover. The cast iron it was made from was heavy. A roaring sounded from below. He rolled onto his back and kicked at the cover with his boots. It was half over the hole when a jet of flame shot out, like the flare-off at an oilrig. Mike kicked the cover again. It clanged into place and Mike lay there panting.

He wiped his hands on the tarmac. Right, so whoever it was knew that investigators had arrived, while he still had no idea as to the source of the problem. He'd better go and report how he had bungled this one.

He was in year five at the college, and he knew he'd never be experienced enough to pass the dreaded year five exam. He rolled over onto his knees and got to his feet. He picked up the coat between a finger and thumb and headed off to report.

Thankfully it was the middle of the night—there was no one on Cavendish Street to smell him. He walked back to the deserted carpark on Aluson Street, and slipped through to the toilet block, where he washed as much as was practical. The legs of his blue jeans remained splashed with filth. With cleaner hands, he finger-combed his shoulder-length brown hair back into a ponytail—a style copied from Trewithick. He checked the time, twenty to three, then fastened his watch back onto his wrist.

The water spiraled down the plughole.

The sewage works, he thought. *Could that be that where the maintenance robots are controlled?*

He trotted over to where the two cars were parked in a corner. The internal light was on in Dunkley's people carrier. The two men sat in the back around a little table that held Dunkley's laptop. Trewithick frowned at the screen while sipping from a neon orange plastic cup. Dunkley looked like he was transferring Internet data from his mobile phone to the laptop, which was odd because Mike knew Dunkley had a mobile connection on his computer.

He tapped on the door and stood back. He would bet he stank.

Trewithick looked up and back at the screen. Then he slid open the door. A dog head poked out round the gap, took a sniff at Mike and pulled back inside, sneezing.

'Well, Mike what's to report?' Trewithick said.

'I managed to set light to the sewer system,' Mike admitted.

Dunkley sat back in his seat. He slipped his mobile into his pocket. Mike flicked him a glance, and could see the amusement in his hazel eyes.

'I'm sure it's not that bad,' Dunkley said. 'We didn't train you to be incompetent.'

Mike gave a wry smile. 'There was a maintenance robot down there. I went to investigate the symbols drawn on it. Then I heard a clicking and remembered about methane.'

'So in fact,' said Trewithick. 'We should be glad you survived an attack. Did you get anything?'

'Not as such, ' Mike said. 'But I wondered if the robots were controlled at the sewage works we saw on the way in. Unless they've out-sourced Maintenance, like everything else these days.'

Trewithick tugged his keys out of his pocket. 'Look Mike, I'm just getting the hang of this computer stuff.' He broke off as Dunkley snorted. 'At least I'm trying. Here, take my van and check out the sewage works, will you?'

Mike fielded the keys tossed to him. 'But I'm all over muck. It'll get on the seats.'

'There's been worse than a little sewage on those seats before now. That's why they're vinyl—it wipes clean.'

'Call us on your mobile if you find anything.' Dunkley turned back to the screen that Mike couldn't see.

Trewithick tugged the sliding door shut and returned to frowning at the screen.

Still reluctant to be operating on his own, Mike trotted over to Trewithick's van. He'd driven both vehicles plenty of times in the past five years when his tutors had ended up too tired or battered by their fights with demonic spirits, but he'd always been with one or other of the two top witch finders. This letting him do some investigating alone puzzled him.

As he tossed his coat onto the passenger seat he realized they must be letting him practice for his year five exams. That was right—they would step in once he phoned them with all the information. With this worked out, Mike relaxed and turned over the engine.

He drove carefully out of Barrow-in-Furness. So what did he know about this situation?

It was likely caused by a fire elemental. He thought that the elemental's human manipulator might be at the sewage works.

Oh and the symbols on the robot were fakes, set to lure a stupid investigator into the firetrap.

Mike pulled up, slightly back from the entrance to the sewage works, and sat for a moment thinking it through. Because of the incident back in town, the perpetrator knew the investigators were on the way. Mike weighed the odds of trying to sneak in the back against just plain walking in the front door. Mike set his mobile phone up with Dunkley's number, now all he had to do was press OK and it would ring out for help. Walk in the front door it was.

Gripping his hiking staff, he set off down the road.

The main gate to the plant was shut at this time of night, but in the building he could see lights on the first floor—presumably where the night operator was working. Mike suspected he was going to look too silly if this man was innocent. It's not like you could just say 'whoops, sorry wrong door' when you were indulging in breaking and entering.

Calming his mind with a simple breath, he said, '*Open me the gates of righteousness.*'

He lifted his staff and lightly tapped the gate. A controlled electrical spark spread out over the gate and found the mechanism.

Mike approved of the well-maintained silence in which they rolled open. Reassured by the thought that by now Mr. Trewithick and Mr. Dunkley would be waiting close by, he strode through.

The door to the building opened to his gentle persuasion. This was very easy and that worried him.

He stepped through the door. To his left was a fire door and an open stairwell, illuminated by the emergency light.

Cautiously, Mike took the stairs up. Even with his heavy boots, his years at the college let him move silently. At the top of the stairs he slid through another fire door and along the corridor.

An open door at the end spewed harsh light into the corridor. Mike crept along. He could hear the clicking of computer keys. It sounded as if whoever was in here could touch type.

Mike stopped. He eyed the floor in front of him, thinking that this was all too easy. Either the perpetrator was somewhere else … or there were some good warnings set out in here.

He breathed some words, '*The ungodly walk on every side, but I shall know the path.*'

More confident, he stepped forward.

On his third step, a jolt of terror ran through him. He moved his foot to one side and the fear subsided. Slowly he approached the open door. He peered through the gap at the hinge side of the open door.

Mike saw banks of computer screens. Most of them showed an image of the sewer system as seen through the camera on a maintenance robot. One screen was blank.

A man sat side on to the door, his hair a greasy ponytail gathered back from a balding head. For a moment his hands stilled on the keyboard. A walking stick leant on the desk beside him. He bent eagerly towards the screen in front of him.

'Come on then!'

For a moment Mike thought the man was talking to him, then guessed that he was talking to the screen.

Pictured was a man with his face half turned away from the screen before him, his lips curled back in a rictus of horror and disgust. Whatever he saw on his screen held him. His eyes widened, and he started panting

'That's it, little man,' said the man in the room. He spun his chair around to face the door. The fluorescent lighting washed all color from his face; he looked like one of those slime moulds from the sewer tunnel. 'Why not come in here? Be in at the death. It's more comfortable, surely, than squinting through that crack.

Damn, Mike thought, *I missed some of the warnings.* Slipping his hand into his pocket, he hit the OK button on his mobile.

'Ah there you are,' said the man. 'I'm Stuart Parry, who are you?'

Mike shrugged.

'It's okay, I suppose. I just like to know who I'm dealing with.' Parry turned back to the screen, licking his lips.

Mike looked at the screen. The victim clenched his fist into the front of his shirt, gasping for breath. Mike had to keep Parry talking until Trewithick and Dunkley arrived.

'Do you know,' Parry said, 'most people are so stupid they don't understand that these liquid crystals in the computer screen are immature water elementals? That's why they align in the way they do by applying electric current.'

'You mean torture them with fire.'

'A simple coercion,' Parry said. 'Every thing works better when it has a reason. The silly thing is that because they fail to understand the nature of what they are working with they torture the poor things until they die, then their screen goes dead and they buy a new one. Watch this now.'

'Stop it!' shouted Mike. 'You're killing him.'

'But that's what we need to do,' said the man. 'I feed my juvenile water elementals on death until they mature. By sending out emails that say that something is wrong with their Internet banking account, I can feed my elementals. It's like the Darwin Awards. The idiots click on the link. That takes them to this video.' Parry waved his hand at a picture from the camera on a maintenance robot. 'Some people even watch to the very end—just to see what's there. Either death to feed the maturing elemental, or the mature elemental will burst out of their computer screen and take them over. I'll soon have an army of them—and incidentally have access to their bank accounts. Let's see if the elemental here is mature enough to break out or whether this will be just another death.'

Mike looked at him in disbelief.

Parry swung round in his chair. 'I thought they'd send one of the big guns after me, but no they've sent a little fifth year on his exam to deal with me.'

'I'm not being examined. Trewithick is just outside.'

The man laughed. 'You don't think they tell you when they are examining you. That's what this is. The fifth year exam is Kill or Be Killed.' He grabbed his stick. '*At the blasting breath of thy displeasure.*'

Lightning spouted from the tip of the stick.

Barely thinking Mike lifted his wrist with watchband turned to Parry.

Reflective surfaces attract lightning. He earthed it, safely, not even damaging the sheen.

'Very good,' said Parry. He waved a hand at the dying man. 'Of course, that was my mistake, why they failed me. One must be able to kill, but one must not enjoy it.'

'*He cast forth lightnings and destroyed them,*' Mike shouted.

Parry lifted a mirror from his pocket, but Mike was not aiming for him. His lightning struck the computer of the sewage works.

On screen the victim took a deeper breath and fell forwards onto his keyboard.

The lightning fail to stop at the computer. It coursed out into the plant. Through the window Mike could see machinery exploding into sparks. He had no time to worry about his uncontrolled lightning.

Parry swung his staff to hit Mike.

Mike dodged around the older man and let the blow hit his shoulders.

Why couldn't he hear Dunkley and Trewithick charging down the corridor?

He swung his hiking stick two-handed at Parry's knee. The force jarred his shoulders, but Parry collapsed onto the ground. With his good foot, Parry kicked back into Mike's shin.

Mike jumped back, looking towards the door.

'Expecting someone?' said Parry. He swung his stick at Mike's groin.

Mike danced away.

Parry got to his feet, favoring one knee. Leaning on his staff, he stood between Mike and the door. 'I told you this is your exam. No one will come until you are dead.'

Parry lunged at Mike. His fingers caught around Mike's throat.

Mike hunched his shoulders and tucked his chin in, his face set in a manic grin as he clenched his teeth to make his neck less vulnerable. He dropped the hiking stick and got his fingers between Parry's hand and the throttling hold on his neck. With his left hand Mike ripped at Parry's sleeve, forcing the hand away from his throat. With as much force as possible, Mike kicked at the older man's damaged knee.

Together they overbalanced and Parry landed on top of Mike, but the hand released the chokehold.

Winded, Mike's sight went black for a moment. He blinked. Parry knelt over him, pulling a knife from a sheath in his sleeve.

Mike punched up into Parry's groin.

Air hissed out of Parry's mouth as he rolled off, curling into a ball.

Panting, Mike pushed to his feet. He reached a hand into his pocket for his mobile. It was quiet. It had dialed and gone silent. Where were his tutors?

Angrily, Mike stabbed the quick dial and called up Dunkley's number again.

Parry burst up from the floor. Using the power of his leap he aimed his knife at Mike's heart.

'Kill or be killed, little fifth year,' Parry shouted.

Mike backhanded Parry. The aerial on his mobile stabbed into Parry's throat. He choked, but still raked the knife down Mike's arm.

It ripped through the waxed cotton of Mike's raincoat. Blood welled up as Mike dodged away, diving for his hiking stick.

Wheezing around the damaged windpipe, Parry tackled Mike to the ground.

Mike twisted and bit Parry's ear. The man howled in pain and fury.

Again Parry reared up to get a good angle for the knife as Mike's fingers scraped his stick.

Mike caught the handle on his stick and swung it around. It whacked Parry in the face.

'*Consume them in thy wrath,*' Mike shouted, thinking of the choking victim.

Parry gasped for air, unable to breathe out. He rolled off Mike onto the floor. Mike got to his feet. Parry weakly punched at his own diaphragm to try and get the air out.

Parry's feet scrabbled on the floor, then he went still. Mike stood over him, his mind blank.

Two sets of footsteps sounded in the corridor. Dunkley and Trewithick walked into the room. Dunkley crouched by Parry and put two fingers to his neck pulse.

'He said… he said.' Mike couldn't get his thoughts around speech.

'He's dead,' said Dunkley. He stood and looked at Mike. Then he reached into his coat and pulled out his wallet. He slipped out a business card with only a cross printed on it. He held it out to Mike. 'Here put this in his hand.'

Mike lifted a shaking hand. To receive the card he would have to reach across Parry's body. Mike shied away and dropped into the computer operator's chair.

He buried his face in his hands, but saw Trewithick bend to fit the card into Parry's hand. Dunkley strode across to the computer station.

'He... Parry said that the fifth year exam is killing someone,' Mike said.

Trewithick shook his head. 'Not always. Bringing someone in for correction is just fine. He believed what he wanted to believe.'

'How can you be so blasé?' Mike shouted. 'I just killed him!'

Trewithick sighed. 'How many people have you had to kill, Dunkley?'

Dunkley kept his eyes firmly on the computer he was analyzing. 'Forty seven.'

'You keep count!'

'No,' said Dunkley. 'I remember everyone I couldn't save.'

Trewithick kept his eyes locked onto Mike's. 'Think of this. Dunkley is remarkable among us for how few people he has killed.'

Mike opened his mouth to ask how many Trewithick had killed, then closed it again. He broke the eye lock and looked down at Parry's corpse. 'But he was one of us!'

Dunkley swung around from his examination of the computer screens. 'What makes you think we have the monopoly on virtue?'

Mike glared back. 'Because our cræft is an inherent part of us—you taught me that—not the gift of an amoral outside force. We debase our souls if we do bad things with it.'

Trewithick patted Mike on the shoulder. 'Think that for as long as it gives you comfort.'

Mike hated the implication of that remark, and was about to say so, then...

'The victim,' he shouted. 'We've got to find out who he was. He needs help.' He jumped up, rummaging in the mess on the desk to see if Parry left any notes lying around.

Both Dunkley and Trewithick relaxed.

'We were monitoring your progress,' said Dunkley.

'When you broke the link and stopped the man from dying,' said Trewithick, 'we sent out a call for an ambulance; it will have arrived at the man's house by now. He'll be fine.'

'Which,' said Dunkley, tapping the computer terminal, 'is more than can be said for this sewage works. The damage is more than I can fix, we'd better alert the maintenance crew.'

'On the bright side,' said Trewithick. 'You passed your fifth year exam.'

Games People Play

Penny stood in the doorway, trying not to be noticed. It was a game she was normally good at, but tonight she felt as if her flaming cheeks shouted her embarrassment to the whole street. And she still had to meet up again with Kelley and stay at her house tonight.

At the moment she hated Kelley. She deserved that Penny just leave her in the West End and drive home.

'It's Penny Bailey, isn't it?'

Penny looked up. She saw a man with light brown hair standing under a street lamp. He was dressed in a long, black coat and heavy boots. The streetlight glinted off the metal hiking stick he carried in his left hand.

She shifted her handbag and slid a hand in to rummage amongst the mess. Her fingers identified the anti-spike drink caps and the pocket breathalyzer that her guardian had given her along with her first car. There it was. Her hand clenched over the highly illegal spray can of mace.

A black taxi whizzed past, but otherwise the street was empty of cars. There were some people, but mostly drunk, even this early in the evening.

Penny considered making a run for it, back to the club she had just stormed out of. The bouncers would surely protect her.

He stepped a little closer. 'Hi! It's Mike Rider, remember we met a few years ago when...'

His voice trailed off as he remembered the full extent of that meeting. Penny remembered it well. Her father had been killed in a freak storm—so the papers said.

She forced a smile. 'I should have recognized you. Karl is always dressed in Van Helsing get up these days.' She gestured at his coat. 'Is it the in-fashion this year at your Uni.?'

'Ah yes, St. Van Helsing College is our nickname, a gift from the other theological colleges.' Mike smiled tightly, as if the joke wasn't to his taste. 'Are you meeting your brother? It's his birthday today isn't it?'

'Half brother,' said Penny.

Mike shrugged. 'If I tried working out all the relationships in your extended family, I'd be here all night. Are you meeting him?'

Penny heard the urgency in his voice.

'I certainly hadn't planned to,' said Penny. 'But I just saw him heading into a Speed Dating session.'

Mike blinked. 'I thought those were for people who were serious about wanting a committed relationship.'

Across the street, a car pulled up in front of the Eden Club, in the no-parking zone. The driver ostentatiously locked the steering wheel with one of those steering locks, then climbed out and deliberately set the anti-theft alarm. Penny could see the penguin-suited bouncer striding down the steps towards the man.

Looking back at Mike, Penny said, 'Are you supposed to be meeting them?'

Mike's eyebrows lifted. 'I'm in my last year—post grad. I'm hardly going to be fraternizing with the first years. No, the reason I'm out here on the pavements, instead of sitting in my study pouring over my dissertation, yet again, is that when I went down to use the library I found the undergrad common room empty. I got a really bad feeling about it. After seven years study at this University you tend to trust those sorts of feeling, you know?'

'Actually,' said Penny, 'I don't know. You don't admit *lady students* into your sacred halls. Something to do with inappropriate plumbing, I understand.'

Mike grinned. 'That has to have been Dunkley who told you that. It certainly sounds like his sense of humor.' His grin faded. 'Look can we deal with your offended feminism later. They're in trouble.'

Across the street Penny could hear the driver starting an argument with the Eden Club bouncer. She knew that voice.

'More than you think,' said Penny. 'That's Kelley's Dad, Steven.'

Mike looked at where the bouncer was trying to placate Steven. 'And who is Kelley?'

Penny grimaced. 'She's the one who dragged me into London after telling her parents we were going to attend a piano recital or some other nonsense. I think he might have just checked her Internet history.'

'Is that where you saw Karl go in?' Mike studied the scene. 'That fracas will make it easier to sneak us in.'

Penny looked at him from under her lashes. 'Sneak? Why should I sneak? I got a ticket.' Penny dug her hand into her pocket and pulled out the crumpled Speeding Ticket. 'I didn't buy it.'

Mike looked between the ticket and the door. 'Hmmm.'

'Do you really expect me to go in there?' asked Penny.

Mike looked up at her face, his eyes wide and innocent. 'They'll need you to keep their numbers straight.'

'I could get into real trouble going back in there. Kelley lied about my age, she said I was eighteen.'

'Aren't you?'

'Not for another two months.'

'Well, don't drink any alcohol then,' Mike said absently. 'Come on, while the other doorman is checking out your ticket, I can sneak in. You do want me to help your bro… half-brother don't you?'

Mike looked at her intently.

Penny rolled her eyes. 'Of course I do. My guardian, his dad would get real upset if any more bad things happened to him.'

She might not get on too well with her half brother, after all he could enter *that* University and she couldn't, but it didn't mean she wanted any harm to come to him. She hitched her handbag over her shoulder more comfortably.

'Let's get on with it then. Can you stop Steven from noticing me as I walk past?'

Mike tutted. 'You were doing fine yourself when I saw you on the street, but okay. *For I am a stranger with thee.*'

Walking across to the Club, Penny said, 'That sounded Bible-ly.'

'Book of Common Prayer,' he muttered.

'Does the Church know you're using Common Prayer to make spells?'

Mike grimaced. 'They're *not* spells, they're mnemonics to focus the mind on the desired result. Common Prayer is very easy to remember in a hurry. What with two services on a Sunday plus Wednesdays and sometimes Fridays you get to memorize large chunks. Believe me, at eight o'clock on winter Wednesday morning you want to be able to sleeptalk your way through the service.'

'*What* are you studying there?'

'A Doctorate of Theology,' Mike whispered. 'Now shut up, you're supposed to be alone.'

Penny clenched her lips as she passed Steven.

'I'm not paying to go in there,' he shouted. 'I just want to go in and get my daughter out.'

'Is she over eighteen?'

'Well, yes of course.'

'Then it's entirely her decision to enter this club,' said the bouncer. 'And not get dragged out by over-protective parents.

Penny turned her face away and produced her Speeding Ticket. The second bouncer smiled. 'Go right in, ma'am.'

Mike was nowhere to be seen. She frowned and looked around, turning like a bull that needed to look at you with both eyes. She squinted. Was he over there?

She saw the shadow Mike watching the row at the entrance. He looked back at Penny then wiped a finger over his lips and flicked it at her. Penny's spine felt shivery. Something had happened there. She took one step towards Mike, but someone grabbed her arm.

'Where have you been?' Kelley demanded.

'Ladies,' Penny muttered.

The shadow Mike was gone.

'Oh for heavens sake,' Kelley said. 'I brought you here to stop you moping over that cousin of yours. A lot of people in the sixth form think you should grow up and stop daydreaming about him as a boyfriend.'

They had discussed her behind her back! Penny was stunned. And then Kelley had invited her home for the Easter Holidays and brought her into London for this stupid Speed Dating night.

Storming back out of the club wasn't an option with Karl in danger.

That reminded her of the danger at the door. She turned to Kelley to warn her about her father being at the door, but what came out was,

'I hope I've got fresh breath for all these meetings.'

Damn him! Mike had put a silence on her! So okay, he didn't want her telling Kelley about her dad, but he could have just asked. Instead he treated her as if she was some silly girlie.

Kelley dragged Penny across the opulent foyer, decorated in green velvet with murals of some romantic ideal of the Garden of Eden. Well, there was a snake in here somewhere.

Kelley ignored the shouting at the doorway, and rummaged in her pocket. 'Here try this.' She offered Penny some chewing gum.

Reluctantly Penny took it. Those inane words that Mike had put in her mouth made it impossible to refuse. She folded the gum into her mouth and let Kelley lead her into the event area.

A woman met them at the door, with a mysterious, tight-lipped smile. Behind her stood a man who epitomized tall, dark and handsome. For once Penny was glad that she was a bit smitten with her cousin Philip, her half brother's half brother. As Mike had said, her family got complicated.

Kelley's chin muscles had melted, drool ran down her chin.

'Welcome ladies, to this Speed Dating event. My name is Marianne. I'm your hostess for this evening. I hope you enjoy your meetings. A complimentary cocktail for you?'

She gave a knowing smile to the man beside her. He lifted two glasses containing neon drinks and offered them to Penny and Kelley. Kelley took hers with an attempt to stroke the man's hand—he seemed good at evading that sort of contact. Penny took the glass with her fingertips; she could see the alcohol hazing off the surface. Her eighteenth birthday had never seemed so far away.

She was about to hand it back and ask for orange juice, when she felt something brush her shoulder. Guessing it was Mike, she moved out into the room to aid his covert entry.

Looking around Penny saw three other people who didn't seem to fancy the neon drink and she dumped her glass on the nearest level surface. With Kelley left behind trying to chat up the hostess's companion, she slipped the foil wrapper of the chewing gum out of her pocket and spat the sticky goo out. She looked around for a bin, but there were none obvious. She doubled wrapped it in the paper and slid it into the front pocket of her handbag.

At the door Marianne frowned and looked to the entrance of the club. She nodded at someone in the room then withdrew, closing the door behind her.

And there was Karl dressed in his darkest Van Helsing get up. Like the poseur he was, he darkly stalked across the room towards her. Penny was finally glad of the Speed Dating event—here was a prime opportunity to get at him.

'Hi Karl,' she said, doing her finest interpretation of a sunbeam.

'What are you doing here?' he hissed.

'I'm trying to get over a certain spell. You know, the love charm on Philip and me? Perhaps you remember the one?' she said. 'How about you? After all this is an event for people who are looking for serious liaisons. Oh and Happy Birthday. I didn't send a card.'

'The charm wasn't like it was meant for you,' Karl muttered.

'No,' said Penny. 'You explained that you intended to use it on your step-sister, Alice.'

Karl went bright red. 'You're too young to be here.'

Penny shrugged. 'I know, but I met Mike Rider in the street just now, he needed me to create a distraction so that he could sneak in ... to look for you I think he said.'

'Mike Rider!' Karl's flush faded fast. 'You never let him in here! He's as prudish as Mr. Dunkley!'

Penny smiled, but only malice touched her eyes.

Karl darted looks around the room.

'You're having me on.'

'If thinking that makes you happy...,' she said, patted his leather-clad shoulder. 'I think we're starting.'

The room door burst open.

'I am going in there,' shouted Steven.

Penny saw Kelley slip through a staff-only door hidden behind a plant. Penny ducked behind Karl.

'Be talking to me,' said Penny. 'But don't let him see me. He'll know his daughter's here otherwise.'

Marianne and a bouncer followed closely. The bouncer grabbed Steven by the wrist, twisted his arm behind him and muscled him out of the room.

Marianne smiled at them all. 'I apologize for that interruption, folks.' She raised a glass of neon cocktail and toasted the room without drinking. 'I hope you find blind love.'

'Well, that was an odd thing to say.' Penny turned back to Karl, his eyes had glazed over.

Surreptitiously, she looked at everyone else in the room. Most of the participants had that same glazed look. The three people Penny had noticed without drinks smirked at each other.

Oh-oh! I think Steven's not the only one in trouble.

Penny decided that since Mike was in here, she ought to go after Steven. What was it Mike had said? Mnemonics to focus the mind. Trouble was, morning assemblies at her exclusive ladies school had never included Common Prayer, just hymns Ancient and Modern.

'Enjoy your evening,' Marianne said, backing out of the room.

Fine, Penny thought. *I'll bet the words don't matter, just the focus. So how about I use hymns?*

'*Light indescribable hiding thy Glory*,' she whispered and stepped quietly to the exit. No one looked at her as she slipped through the closing door.

The thick carpet in the entrance lobby muffled her footsteps. Marianne stalked across the foyer, flinging open another *staff only* door. Again Penny managed to slide through.

It was an office. She sneaked along the wall, out of the way.

Steven was dumped in a chair. His hair was ruffled and one of his cheeks glowed red in a way that suggested a later bruise. Buttons were torn from his shirt and his hands were cuffed in front of him. The metal dug into his wrists as he struggled to free them.

Marianne sat behind the desk and stared at Steven over her hands, held in a curious prayer-like fashion.

'Don't worry, Steven,' Marianne said. 'I'm going to reunite you with your daughter. She left the meeting room somewhat abruptly, but we will find her.'

Penny felt a shiver down her spine that had nothing to do with magic. She saw Marianne frown in her direction and started to squint. Penny concentrated on her words. She needed to remain unseen. Marianne shook her head and regarded at Steven.

'You can't do this to me,' he shouted.

'Oh yes we can,' said Marianne. 'We are detaining a violent man suspected of being…' She clicked her fingers and stood up. 'The alcohol, there's always something to forget.'

She sashayed over to cabinet on the wall. Inside was a bottle of that neon cocktail. When she unscrewed the lid, Penny smelled the increased alcohol content of the air from across the room.

'When we turn you over to the police, you'll be so drunk no one will believe a word you say.'

'I never drink spirituous liquor,' said Steven. 'I'm a Church Warden. No one would believe I'd drunk that.'

Marianne poured out a glassful. 'It's amazing what people will believe. Your smugness tells me there are people who will enjoy your downfall into sin. You see, you're going to kill your daughter in a furious rage. We have a lot of witnesses to your breaking in here.'

A tap on the door. 'Come.'

The bouncer dragged in Kelley. Well, dragged only in the sense that the bouncer had to hold off her attempts to furiously kiss him.

'We found her on the dance floor,' said the bouncer, smirking. 'And had to remove her for licentious behavior.'

Hah! thought Penny. *That drink's a love charm. Let's see how Karl likes it.* Penny fought the urge to get out her mobile and email a picture of Kelley's debauch to all their friends.

Marianne glared at Kelley. 'That's enough! Stand still!'

Kelley became a living statue.

Oh! It's only a control charm, thought Penny.

'Now let's…'

'There's just one more thing, ma'am,' said the bouncer.

'Go on.'

'There's another girl missing from the Speed Dating session,' said the bouncer. 'And one of the *others* found a full glass of cocktail.'

Marianne looked thoughtful, while Penny held her breath again.

'Have the *others* selected their Dinner Dates?'

'Yes ma'am.'

'Good!' said Marianne. 'Bring worried Papa over here and hold him down.'

Penny frowned. Steven had a paunch and was a tall man, but the bouncer lifted him with no effort at all, despite his struggles.

'Kelley,' screamed Steven. 'Run!'

Kelley was oblivious to the molestation of her father. Penny felt sick. She wondered why she had come in here to watch this. There was nothing she could do. The bouncer laid Steven on the desk and held him in place across the oak veneer.

'Stop this,' Steven shouted. 'I demand that you let my daughter and I go!'

'No!' Marianne looked amused. She held the glass of neon cocktail up to Steven's lips. 'Drink all the nice medicine, now. Perhaps this will teach you not to jump in where you are unwanted.'

Steven turned his head to one side and the fluorescent liquid tipped into his ear. He shook his head. Marianne caught Steven by the nose and held it closed, like a nurse forcing a recalcitrant child to open their mouth for yummy castor oil.

Steven gasped. 'Stop this…'

The cocktail went into his mouth. He spat out orange gunk.

'Lie still,' Marianne commanded.

Steven stopped struggling.

'That's a good Papa,' Marianne crooned. 'Drink all of this now.'

It was a huge glass, much larger than the complementary cocktail Penny and Kelley had received.

'Now, carry Papa into the Dining Room. He can be my Date. Kelley, come along now.' She ran a finger over her lips. 'I'm really looking forward to Dinner tonight.'

Kelley followed Marianne as the bouncer picked up the quiescent Steven. Penny followed them out of the office. Witnessing the activities seemed to be all she could do for the moment. Until she could figure out who she was supposed to report this to.

They returned to the room where they had started the evening. The lights were lowered now. The bouncer dumped Steven on his feet in the middle of the floor. Even under the control spell, he wobbled from the effect of all that alcohol.

The Speed Dating session was over. Six people waited for them. The three non-drinkers from the pre-date meeting, two men and one woman, stood beside human statues. The woman had chosen Karl.

Marianne waved an arm, and some frenzied music started playing. 'Let's dance.'

She claimed Steven as her dance partner. The bouncer grabbed Kelley, pulling her against him. From where she stood by the door Penny was horrified. Dirty Dancing had nothing on this. The music wove magical strands of frantic seduction. Penny shrank away from this parody of love. The club dancers bent towards their prey, smiling broadly.

And Penny could see their teeth.

They're vampires. Penny wanted to scream. Suddenly she saw Mike Rider. He knelt on the floor with hands covering his ears.

Marianne saw Mike too. She dropped Steven, who collapsed to the floor, and walked with swaying hips towards Mike.

This was too much for Penny. She screamed out, *'Brave Redeemer come and heal us.'* Sharp spikes drove into her head, but she continued. *'Calm our souls, quell all desires.'*

Feeling week and dizzy Penny dropped to her knees.

With a wave of Mike's hand, the music stopped. He jumped up to face Marianne.

Penny knew her eyes were acting up. She thought she saw Marianne's hands growing into claws.

Mike braced his feet and swung his staff, whacking Marianne upside the head.

Marianne's neck bent at an impossible angle under the blow. Penny was sure heard a snap. Her corpse skidded across the floor from the force of the blow. Penny skittered back on her knees to stop the head from touching her. She looked at it, then up at Mike, horrified at how casually he had killed.

Mike glanced in her direction. 'Do nothing more, Penny. Leave this to me.' He turned to deal with the three subordinate creatures now bearing down on him.

'It's a witch finder,' said the woman. 'How did he get in here without an invitation.'

Mike smiled. 'One of your guests invited me in.'

Well, if you loosely interpreted her words, they could comprise an invitation. Penny rubbed her temples; her head ached, which was unfair, because she'd drunk nothing this evening.

In a dream, she watched Mike casually swat the creatures that attacked him

Mike shouted, *'There was a smoke that went out in his presence and a consuming fire out of his mouth.'*

Penny watched as the creatures coughed. Smoke erupted from their mouths and they screamed in pain.

At her knee, Marianne wriggled. Penny's mouth dropped open as she watched the neck straighten. Whatever spirit possessed Marianne must be healing her. Penny checked on Mike but he was fully occupied with the three attacking him. It was up to her to do something.

Spirits, she thought dreamily.

Remembering Steven and his spirituous liquor, she slipped her hand into her handbag and produced the pocket breathalyzer that her guardian had bought her. He had strict ideas about not drinking and driving, probably from his own life and … Penny regained control of her rambling thoughts.

Oh that would be too easy! But she had to try something.

She put the mouthpiece of the breathalyzer between Marianne's lips and said, *'Sin cast out by Angels Holy.'*

More pain stabbed through her eyes from behind. The colors in the room faded into monochrome, but she held onto the thought. The digital dial counted a large amount of alcohol in the breath. It flashed out a danger warning.

Marianne's skin turned white and papery. And bits of the fancy suit collapsed.

'What's happening?' she whispered. Looking up she could see that Mike was finishing off the last of his attackers. Penny dropped her gaze back to Marianne.

Her skin was crumbling into powder.

Mistiness was creeping out of the mouthpiece. The spirit mustn't escape. Penny looked around for something to stopper the breathalyzer. She scrabbled through her handbag, tipping it upside down on the floor. Among all the junk a small paper wrapped bundle fell out.

The chewing gum, thought Penny, *the very thing.*

She unwrapped the soggy mess and shoved it up the mouthpiece, whispering, '*Sin condemned thee, sealed thy fate.*'

She barely got the words out before the walls tumbled in on her.

The dizziness was still there when the light registered on the other side of her eyelids. She kept them shut.

'Are you sure she'll be all right?' Karl's voice felt like a blackjack clubbing her head. 'My Dad'll kill me if anything happens to our Penny. Social Services have never been too keen on him being her guardian.'

Penny screwed her eyes open a touch. She saw curtains and heard footsteps briskly tapping past on the other side.

'Ah! The dead awaken,' Mike said. 'I told you not to do any more.'

'What happened?' she whispered. Even her own voice echoed in her head.

'Why do you think *we* are taught so slowly?' asked Mike. 'We have to build up our tolerance for the energy drain. You went into hypoglycæmia.'

She could see a drip in her arm.

'I phoned Dad to tell him which hospital we're at,' said Karl appearing in her vision. 'He's on his way down from Yorkshire. I think he's hired a helicopter.'

'Can't he just be a normal person for once?' moaned Penny.

'What? You expect Dad to act normally?' asked Karl. 'He's the guardian to the daughters of his two ex-wives.'

Penny frowned as she remembered the evening. 'Mike, how come I only felt disgusted by the love charm? It even flattened you.'

Mike snorted. 'You're lucky in one respect. The charm Karl here put on you cancels out all others—until you really fall in love.'

Karl hunched his shoulder and glared. 'Gonna get a drink.' He slouched out, since curtains can't slam, he flicked them aggressively back into place.

Penny flicked a glance at Mike. 'I killed her, didn't I?'

Mike smiled slightly. 'You know Penny, now would be a good time to cultivate a bad memory. I'm expected to kill infested persons, if I can't save them. You could get into a lot of trouble saying it was you.'

Mike held up the breathalyzer. 'Now this is a novel idea. Mr. Dunkley is going to want to talk to you.'

Night Watchman

Blood-red light falls on Mike's hands. Lifting his gaze, he realizes it is dawn. The rising sun shines through the red cross in the stained glass window. He follows the path of the light up from his hands, to where it spills off the long sword, lying on the altar. The sword he is supposed to take up today.

Once, long ago, something bad happened. In his travel journal, Julius Caesar claimed to be horrified at what was happening when the Romans arrived to take a look at their future possession. But he must have known why.

It's easy to make mistakes.

Mike has knelt here all the short summer night, remembering.

Mike had watched them. He lay behind a boulder, wrapping the night around his shoulders like a familiar coat. Just another group requiring a tick in the box labeled *harmless*.

Out on the beach, they had fuel for a bonfire. And there was the obligatory Wickerman, woven from willow, facing the five miles of unspoiled beach. The Solstice Revelers pulled their white robes over jeans and suits. By day they were pillars of the community, lawyers and doctors, but at night they played with Fire.

Mike studied the model through his binoculars, wondering if the celebrants were going to burn it or toss it out to sea. They dragged the Wickerman to below the high water mark and piled faggots of wood and sheaves of straw around it.

Ah! thought Mike, *they're going to burn it and let the ashes wash out to sea.*

He put down his binoculars to make a note on his assessment form. A movement on the beach caught his attention. He snatched up his binoculars again.

What is that? Mike adjusted the focus. To one side they held a man, tied up, wearing only shorts. And watching it all, away from the fire a woman and her two boys.

'*Carry my words to the hills,*' whispered Mike.

'Don't worry, Daniela,' said the bound man, his words flying on the night breeze to Mike's ears. 'I've got to do this for you, and the boys.'

Daniela looked between the bonfire and the man.

'No, Greg,' she said. 'We've managed—we will manage.'

The vestry door opens and Trewithick enters the chapel, dressed in the white knee-length tabard of his calling. A simple red cross, identical to the one in the stained-glass window, is embroidered across the left shoulder.

Roman writers said that human sacrifice was a part of the Celtic religion. Why it should have horrified them, Mike has never understood. They held their gladiatorial games—fights to the death in honor of this or that god from the Roman pantheon.

But by this they justified the slaughter of the Druids: man, woman and child. No more placatory rituals were performed for the worst spirits driven out of Europe onto the British Isles. Leaving only the Wizard-Smiths to contain them, with stone, iron and salt.

On the beach a drum started. The group solemnly circled sunwise around the fire. Lifting their arms, they chanted something indistinguishable to Mike. Greg fell to his knees.

Daniela held the smallest of her boys close, turning his face into her shoulder. The older boy watched with wide-open eyes.

Two of the hooded celebrants lifted Greg by the shoulders to his feet. He staggered as they walked him forward.

Mike pocketed his binoculars; they clattered against the gun in his pocket. He hadn't expected this sort of thing in Worthing.

In the chapel, Trewithick lays out the altar for the service: the silver chalice, the plate, the white cloth. Everything set out in the red light of a new dawn.

Tears leak down Mike's face as he remembers what happened next.

Mike watched them tie Greg to the spike holding the Wickerman upright. Around him and the Wickerman, the celebrants piled more wood and straw. The chanting took on a more urgent tone. The circle expanded, including Greg tied to the pole as well as the main fire. The revelers each picked up a torch and lit it at the main fire. They circled closer and closer to the Wickerman, waving their flaming brands at the unlit fire. Greg cringed away from them, turning his face from the flames.

Daniela buried her face in the hair of her youngest child.

A spark dropped into the tinder at Greg's feet. His mouth opened in a soundless scream. His arm muscles bulged as he tried to snap his bonds. Someone thrust a flaming torch into the fuel at his feet.

This had gone too far. Mike jumped to his feet, dropping his shadows. He charged into the firelight.

Lifting his hand high he shouted, '*But thou delightest not in burnt offerings.*'

As he dropped his hands all the flames on the beach died. Greg looked up and smiled at Mike.

The leader of the circle tore off his hood and flung it to the ground. 'You idiot,' he shouted. 'You stupid little witch finder. We had nearly got the demon out of him.'

'You don't drive out demons that way.' Mike put his face into the leader's. 'If there is a demon in that man, you will have only angered it.'

'We would have got it out.'

'But there is a demon,' said Daniela. She stood and walked across to the arguing men.

A patronizing smile drifted across Mike's face. 'You mean they've told you there is a demon. Demonic infestation is really quite rare. What does he do? Get angry? Hit you?'

'No,' said Daniela.

'Dad turns into this huge bear,' said the older boy.

Mike spun around. 'You fools! You've been baiting a bear!'

A sharp crack rang through the night.

'Edward!' shouted one follower. 'It's breaking free.'

Greg had broken the pole to which the chains and ropes bound him. He pawed away the broken ends and the ropes and chains fell away. Free now, the man's hair grew and he charged the circle of people. Claws sprouted from his paws. The woman clutched at her sons and shrank away.

The manbear turned to where Mike and Edward stood in confrontation. It towered over the six-foot Edward and clawed the air. Mike ducked under the paws, and rolled back to his feet behind the bear. Edward was less prepared. A plate-sized paw swiped him across the face, flinging him to the ground. Still Edward tried to wriggle away.

Hovering by the fire Mike shouted, 'Play dead for a bear!'

The bear dropped his front paws onto Edward. Mike thought he heard the crack of snapping spine. The manbear growled as it savaged an arm.

Mike assessed the situation very quickly. He had to lure the bear away from the revelers. He sprinted towards Daniela. Grabbing the oldest boy, he slung him over his shoulder like a sack.

'Run!' he ordered.

The soft sand tripped his feet. He heard more screams behind him. From beyond the beach he heard a car engine start, then a squeal of tires.

Once across the beach, he started up the gully. Looking back, he hoped that the tactic of stealing its mate and cubs would get the bear to give chase. It was distracted by the other potential prey, but was moving in the right direction.

Daniela followed about ten meters behind Mike, cuddling her younger child to her chest.

Mike heaved the boy he was carrying over the gate.

'Keep running,' he shouted at the boy as he turned back to help the mother.

'Do you know anywhere safe?' he gasped as he wrenched the younger boy out of her arms.

'How about a car?' she shouted.

'Great idea,' Mike said. 'Shame I brought my motorbike.'

'My car's that way,' the woman said. She pointed up the gully.

Reaching the gate, Mike lowered the younger boy down on the other side while the woman climbed over. With a glance over his shoulder, he vaulted the gate and hefted the younger child over his shoulder. Behind them at the dead fire, the beast roared as its tormentors scattered into the night and turned to retrieve its mate.

The older boy hovered near by. The woman stopped on the other side, digging into her pocket for her keys. Gritting his teeth Mike snatched them, tossing them to the older boy.

'Run!' he shouted.

The boy hared up the road. Mike raced after him, carrying the younger boy. Behind him, he heard the woman's walking boots thumping erratically.

Along the edge of the road a number of cars were drawn up onto the verge of the narrow lane.

The lights on a car two in front of Mike came on and the engine started. Hoping it was the older boy, Mike shifted the younger boy under one arm. He yanked open the rear door and stuffed the boy into a child seat.

Behind him, the woman tugged on the driver door as the older boy scrambled into the passenger seat.

Mike slammed the back door. 'Right,' he said. 'Get away now!'

The woman leant against her side of the car. 'Why did you stop them?' she asked.

'Because that's not the way to drive out an infestation,' said Mike.

'And how would you know?'

The older boy stared out of the window at Mike. 'The leader called this man a witch finder. Are you here to hunt Dad?'

'I'm here to check out this group. We have to keep an eye on all those who work with true Cræft.'

'And just who is this *we*?' asked the woman.

'The Church of England,' said Mike. 'Now stop talking and go!'

'And what can you do?'

At the bottom of the lane another person scrambled over the gate. The manbear smashed through the weathered wood behind him.

Mike spun around. 'Dammit woman, get your kids out of here.'

She got into the car and started maneuvering her car out of the line parked on the grass verge.

Mike ducked behind the line of cars watching the beast.

Behind him, the engine stalled.

Glancing over his shoulder he saw Daniela frantically turning the key. The engine sputtered. Shung, shung, shung sounded from the flooded starter motor.

'I may not be packing for bear but I'll do my best.' Reluctantly, Mike pulled out the handgun. He broke it open and dumped the regular bullets onto the ground. He looked at the moon and saw it was at three-quarters. From another pocket he produced the other bullets, the silverplated ones. With trembling hands, he aimed a bullet at the chamber.

A handgun was the last thing to use against an enraged bear—for an accurate shot, he needed to get close.

The furious creature lifted a car and shoved it into the ditch. Then it dropped on all fours to charge up the lane.

He'd managed to get one bullet into the gun before the bear rammed its head into its wife's car.

The car crashed against another; the alarm blared into the night. The driver door popped open and Daniela was flung from the car into the road. The rear wheels of the car slid slowly into the ditch.

Momentarily dazed by the jolt, the manbear stood shaking its head.

Shutting the gun, Mike scrambled back along the lane. One bullet would have to be enough.

Mike got between Daniela and the dazed bear. Remembering his lessons, he planted his feet firmly on the tarmac road and lifted his gun to aim.

Behind him, he heard Daniela's boots scrape on the tarmac as she stood.

'You're not killing my husband!'

She yanked on his arm trying to reach the gun. Mike raised his arm above his head, keeping the gun out of reach.

'It's the only way,' said Mike. 'I can't leave that monster rampaging through the countryside. The demon will have completely taken over because of its treatment tonight.'

'No!' she screamed. 'My husband is still in there. He will come back. He's always come back before.'

Daniela lifted her knee. Mike jerked backwards, keeping his groin safe. She jammed her heavy walking boot down on his instep instead.

Mike swore under his breath, still trying to hold her back. She shoved on his shoulders. Off balance from the first unexpected attack, he staggered. She tore free of his grasp and ran over to the bear.

'Greg!' she shouted.

Mike lifted the gun again; Daniela deliberately got in the way.

He moved into the shadow of the hedge and behind another car, getting behind the bear. The hawthorn branches scratched at him through the summer-weight shirt.

'Greg,' she said. 'Greg!'

She held out her arms to the manbear. It stopped shaking its head and stumbled towards her. She stepped forwards.

'Greg, I love you, come back,' she said, voice quivering. 'The boys need their dad.'

The beast shambled towards her and snuffled the air. Mike froze, wrapping the scent of the night around him. The woman dropped to her knees to look in the bear's eyes.

'Greg? I know you're in there,' she said.

Get out of the way woman. Mike took one noiseless step, and then another.

The bear closed in on her. Suddenly, the creature reared up on two legs again. It pounded the ground in a display of dominance. Mike gnawed on his bottom lip. Could the creature recognize its mate?

'Be submissive,' Mike breathed, letting the night air carry his words to her only. 'Lie on your back.'

She lay on her side and rolled onto her back, leaving her neck exposed. The creature pounded the ground again. Then it lowered its muzzle to her chest. The creature lay down, head pillowed on her breast.

'What now?' she whispered.

'Do you love him?' Mike asked.

'That's a stupid question.'

'Answer me,' Mike hissed.

'Yes, I love him.'

'Are you absolutely sure that he loves you?' Mike asked. 'And be careful of your answer, because your children could be orphans tonight if you are wrong.'

She didn't even hesitate. 'Yes he loves me.'

'Then hold him tightly,' said Mike. 'Don't let him go. No matter what happens. No matter what form he takes. No matter how disgusting or delightful.'

Even in the poor moonlight, Mike saw the woman trembling as she cradled the manbear's head.

'Come back to me, Greg.' She whispered, but Mike could hear. 'Come back! I need you. I love you.'

The bear roared, struggling to free his head, but the woman tightened her grip.

Still holding the night, scent and sight, around him, Mike moved closer. If she let go, or if he was wrong about the situation, he needed to be much closer than this to get an accurate/lethal shot on a bear with a handgun.

The bear shifted. It roared again with the pain of the change. The bear turned into a large rat and Daniela shrieked.

'Don't let go!' Mike said.

'Greg,' she said. Mike saw tears reflecting the moonlight. 'I don't want a rat, I want Greg.'

Mike slipped a finger under his shirt collar and eased out a chain. Lifting the silver crucifix over his head, he tossed it to her.

'Get that over his head,' said Mike. 'If you can.'

She buried her face in the stinking rat fur. A squeal and the creature transformed again. This time it was a slimy slug. It stank as it slithered out of her arms. She gripped tighter, but the slime helped it to slip free. She cradled it, turning her whole body into a cup to contain the slug.

'Greg,' she whispered again.

Next it chose the form of a small kitten. With claws and teeth it tried to fight its way free. She caught it by the scruff. With her free hand she snatched up the chain and hung it around the creature's neck. The kitten squalled in pain. Then she was cuddling a panther.

Mike sank to the ground. Finally he had a chance of a decent shot. Then it was Greg, lying naked in her arms. The crucifix burnt a shadow on his bare chest. Mike heard the flesh sizzling.

'I'm back, Daniela,' said Greg. 'You can let go.'

Mike eased off the safety. Daniela cuddled Greg tightly against her chest. She nestled her head in his shoulder.

'I didn't let you go when you frightened me,' she said. 'I'm not letting you go now.'

The frenzied bear returned, but Daniela held on.

It tried rearing.

But this time, the creature and Greg were equal partners in its head.

It tried biting, but the jaws snatched away, inches from Daniela's throat. And still she clung on.

Mike waited. He ought to fire, but he hoped Greg and Daniela would win.

On the chest of the bear, the crucifix scorched a cruciform. The cross glowed blue in the moonlight, and the fur near the silver smoked.

Then it was the man again. He wrapped his arms around Daniela's shoulders and buried his face in her hair.

Getting slowly to his feet, Mike stepped out of the shadows and walked to the couple in the road. Mike kept his gun pointed at the ground.

'Who's in there?' he asked.

Greg surged to his feet, pulling Daniela with him. Using her as a prop, he ignored his nakedness and glared at Mike.

'What the hell do you think you were doing? I felt it leaving me. They were scaring it out with the fire.'

Mike shrugged 'If you felt anything, you felt it pretending to leave. Despite the press, the threat of burning never drives out a demon—not until the body is scorched and dead.'

'And you know more about it than them!' shouted Greg.

'Yes,' said Mike. 'I'd better go and tidy up the mess on the beach.'

'You set it free!' shouted Greg. 'With your interruption.'

'It was already getting free.' Mike turned away. He learned early that people rarely offered thanks for saving their lives.

Two shadows climbed out of the car that was in the ditch

'Right!' said Greg. 'Then you let my wife take those risks.'

Mike winced; the truth grated on his soul. 'And just how else was I supposed to get you away from all that prey? I'm not meant to be a hero—I've just got to get the job done.'

'Well, I'm cured now. Get out of here,' said Greg.

'No! You're not cured.' Mike lifted the gun and pointed it straight at Greg's heart. Deliberately he slid off the safety. 'This bullet is silver, that will *cure* you.'

Greg pushed Daniela behind him, as she tried to get in the way of the muzzle again.

'At present time,' said Mike, 'you are in charge of your body. You are what we call a berserker.'

'Cool,' said a boy's voice. 'You mean like those Viking warriors who ripped off their armor and charged whole armies in the nudie?'

'Yes, just like that. If you lose your temper, or indeed if you choose to, you will change into a bear at any point. If you love your wife and kids—never remove the chain.'

Mike watched Greg down the barrel of his gun. Then he slid the safety back in place and returned the gun to his pocket. He tossed a white business card at their feet, too angry to care at the discourtesy. 'Phone the number on that card, make an appointment. We can help you, properly.'

'And I'm to trust you more than the folks I know, am I?'

'If you have any sense, yes.' Mike walked back down the lane to the beach.

In the church the chanting begins. Yes, he let the woman take the risks.

Mistakes are easy. Admitting the fault and working to put it right, no matter how long it takes is what counts.

Trewithick lifts the sword that Mike—the latest in the line of Smiths—has made to prove his worth.

Trewithick speaks. 'Will your Duty stand above the rest, never putting one person first?

'I will.'

'Have you the strength to seek knowledge and put it to best use?'

'I have.'

Getting to his feet, Mike takes the sword and holds it aloft. The risen sun now shines through plain glass and bathes him in golden light.

'How stand you on the Night?'

'Against the weak, the lazy and the evil ones who summon the dark, and for the innocents who know nothing of this world, I Stand Watch.'

Ghost Sun

The sun hovered above a fog bank as Alice turned the car into the drive. Sea fret crawled over the cliff edge and swallowed the cottage at the end of a drive that Alice only now discovered was blocked by a five-barred gate.

A few spots of rain spattered on the windscreen among the bugs she had collected on the drive up here. They were quickly followed by a mizzle that blurred the view. She flicked the windscreen wipers, but all that did was smear wet bug blood over the glass.

With a muttered curse, she groped on the floor of the passenger side and found her red folding umbrella. Opening the car door, she shot the umbrella up.

Awkwardly she slid out of the car, avoiding a mud puddle created to ruin her good work shoes.

The drizzle hung in the air now. Her brolly was useless; within moments the gray of her good linen suit was spotting with black.

Two statues leered at her from either gatepost; Pan-like figures frozen mid-pole dance around two lamps erupting from the gateposts. The sea fog roiled down the drive towards her.

Shivering, she walked up to the gate and inspected the latch. A heavy chain and padlock held it shut.

Pushing her short hair from her eyes, she sighed. Overhead the sun, like a ghost eye, made a last effort to burn away the clouds.

Transferring the brolly to her left hand, she reached into her jacket pocket for her mobile. She punched a number with a practiced thumb and held it to her ear. The phone rang, and rang. Putting it away again, she rattled the chain in frustration, hoping that the padlock would spring open.

A yipping bark made her jump.

A fox, its damp coat clumping together in spikes, had climbed on the dry stone wall to the right of the gate and was staring at her. Affronted, Alice stared back.

'You're supposed to be nocturnal,' she said. 'There's still an hour until sunset. So you just back off—I have every right to be here.'

A deeper bark sounded, with an echo. Alice turned to see two wolfhounds bounding down the road looking for sport. The fox fled.

A man with a hiking stick followed the two dogs. A beard shadowed his chin, and a plait of hair hung to his waist. Alice felt her lips curve into a sneer as she recognized him. He lifted an eyebrow, then called to his dogs.

'*Thugain thu.*' His Scottish accent hardly faded when he switched back to English. 'Have we met?'

'I wouldn't say we've been introduced, Mr. Dunkley, but I watched you talking to my cousin, Penny Bailey. It was a few years back,' she added with a shrug.

'Then you would be Alice ... Carsden?'

'Yes, I changed my name when I found out who my father was,' said Alice. 'And that he was the other man killed on that hillside—to stop me being sacrificed.'

'I didn't realize, when I sent him there, that he was your father. Gordon was the only person close enough to help.' Dunkley looked into the distance as he bent to stroke a dog behind the ear. 'I would have visited you, but Penny said you wanted to be left alone.'

'I just want to be normal,' said Alice.

'Then what are you doing here?'

Alice gaped at him. 'Mr. Werlow lives here. He called in sick to the office this morning and he's not answering his phone. I'm his secretary. His partner discovered he'd taken some documents home with him last night. We're defending the man accused of those murders we've been having around here. The files are needed, because we're instructing Counsel tomorrow.'

'Of all the jobs, solicitor's secretary is hardly the one I would have thought that Colin Stempress's step-daughter would take.'

'I said I wanted to be ordinary.' She wrinkled her nose. 'Don't tell me you're a fan?'

Dunkley laughed. 'While I've never been a classical only sort of listener, Glam Rock rarely shows up on my playlist.' He put on hand on the gate, near the hinge, and vaulted over. He turned back to look at her. 'Are you coming then?'

Alice watched the wolfhounds—one of them leapt over the gate, the other wriggled between the bars.

She looked back at Dunkley. 'Can't you do some boogie-woogie magic on the padlock?'

'I don't do *magic*. And no.'

For a moment Alice felt some interest break through her annoyance. 'Is it true that you can't magic, I mean affect, metal?'

'It's just not polite.' He turned away and stared at the neat line of poplars, raised on banks on either side of the long gravel drive, fading into the mist.

Tossing the brolly over, Alice hitched up her pencil skirt and clambered over the gate. She picked up the brolly again and hurried after him.

'I explained my business,' she said. 'What are *you* doing here?'

He had a slight frown between his eyes as he looked back from his study of the fog. 'I'm paying the annual courtesy visit to one of our retired Inspectors.'

'Mr. Werlow was a witch finder!'

'Alice, we are not witch finders. I'm an Inspector for the Church Office of Misuse of Cræft, as was Stan Werlow. He taught me.' Dunkley sighed. 'You make it sound like I work for the Spanish Inquisition. Only people who have unfavorable inspections call us *witch finders*.'

Alice walked on in silence. The gravel crunching underfoot was the only noise in the world. The misty drizzle made her feel a bit deaf around the eyes. Even the grass on the other side of the poplar trees seemed monochromatic, like a moody photograph.

A breeze blew between the poplars and water pattered on the brolly. Alice glanced up, but instead of the expected branches of late leaves she saw cobwebs stretched across the drive: ten feet between the trees.

'Get me if I'm wrong,' said Alice. 'But isn't this feeling a bit Mirkwood?'

Dunkley scanned the trees. 'Banana spiders. I didn't know they had got to this country. They travel with crates of bananas, hence the name. Don't you like spiders?'

More water dripped on them from the webs.

'It's too close to Halloween for me to like spiders,' she muttered.

Dunkley's hazel eyes glinted with laughter but he kept his face straight. 'What's the case that you need the file for?'

Alice shivered again then turned away from the spooky webs. 'It's an old man accused of killing some people who drove his daughter Alison into committing suicide about thirty years ago. He says he had nothing to do with the killings.' Alice shrugged. 'The evidence is a bit circumstantial. They were very ritual, the murders I mean. I was a bit surprised not to see one of you lot up here, but then if Mr. Werlow was one of you, he'd report anything suspicious.'

'You'd think so, wouldn't you?'

The dogs growled and came on alert, running to the edge of the drive. The drifting fog showed the fox pacing next to them. It darted back into the mist.

The mist dulled time; Alice felt she'd been walking for hours in the half-light. Her spine itched, there was something uncanny about the air. She looked out of the corner of her eye, trying to catch the pictures that the mist was trying to build.

'That's not a good idea. Even if you know what you're doing, illusion can trap you.' Dunkley lifted a hand. '*At the brightness of his presence the clouds removed.*'

Alice clutched her brolly as a gust of wind shredded the mist and the sun's pale eye brightened. Her late afternoon shadow stretched back, as if trying to escape to the car.

His mouth twitched into a half smile. 'I was getting sick of the fog. Besides, there were misdirections in it. I hope nothing has happened to Stan.'

A cottage, painted white, stood close to the cliff edge in front of them.

'We could have gone over the cliff edge in that fog!' Alice said.

'I suspect that's what the misdirections were intended to do.'

Dunkley walked to the front door and rapped on the wood with the handle of his hiking stick.

Vertigo washed over Alice. If Dunkley hadn't walked up the drive with her she would have gone over the edge. While the sea was quiet today, it was a fair drop down to the rolling breakers.

To Alice the knock sounded hollow, as if the house were empty. She turned away from the cliff and gazed around. Sea pinks and other salt tolerant plants grew in neat rows along the walls of the cottage. And there, standing on the brick wall, was the fox.

Alice stared into the brown eyes. She heard the laughing of children. They must be playing on the beach below.

'Stan?' Dunkley shouted.

The only answer was the breeze bringing the slosh-splash of the waves up to their ears.

Dunkley set his stick aside and tried the latch.

The door swung open and he stepped the house.

After another glance around the garden, Alice followed him in turning to fold her umbrella before entering.

The door opened directly into a lounge. Dunkley must have passed through already, because the room had no one in it. The sofa had plumped up cushions and there were fresh flowers, picked from the garden, on the driftwood coffee table, standing next to the pile of files tied up in legal ribbon.

Dropping the brolly on the table, Alice picked them up. Checking the labels, she saw they were the ones she needed.

From the back of the house, Alice heard a woman singing and children laughing and screaming in delight; she thought she could hear the squeak of an old swing.

Mr. Werlow had never brought a wife to the office Christmas party. He never mentioned children

Frowning, she walked to the other door.

It led into a tight kitchen. The remains of a sandwich and the dregs of a mug of tea stood in the sink, but there was no one here. The back door was open, as was a second door showing the bottom step of some narrow stairs. The singing was louder through that door.

Curious, Alice put a foot on the steps. Distance blurred the words, but the tune sounded like a lullaby.

The scent of flowers and fresh spring air drifted down the stair, luring Alice. She ran lightly up the steps and into the only bedroom.

For a moment Alice saw a woman bending over a cradle. The woman looked up and smiled. She opened her mouth to speak.

The gust of wind, keeping away the mist outside, blew the curtains at the open window. The shadows shifted.

The rotting wood of the cradle creaked as the breeze from the open window rocked it. On the heavy wooden bed lay a body. The long hair still attached to the skull told her it was a woman. Her skin had mummified, pulled tightly over the skull.

A dent was still in the pillow next to the body. The red satin counterpane covering the bed had been straightened, but not perfectly. The smell of flowers was replaced with moldy mustiness.

Nausea washed over Alice. She slapped a hand to her mouth and stumbled down the stairs. She raced out of the back door and dropped to her knees on the grass, retching dryly.

Then Dunkley crouched next to her, offering a glass of water.

'Did you find him?' he asked.

Alice took a sip of from the glass and shook her head. Tears leaked down her face. 'In the front bedroom. I think he's been sleeping next to... to a...'

Over the sea, the sun was sinking into the sea fog. Off in the distance, she heard a foghorn sounding on the headland.

Dunkley stood and entered the house. Alice realized that she was still carrying the notes.

Using the house wall, she got to her feet and staggered around to the front. She put the notes on the drystone wall, carefully out of the way. She hesitated at the front door, then pushed it open. She felt dizzy as she crossed the threshold. The singing started up again, and the laughter of children.

Dunkley walked through from the kitchen. His face was set into a grim line. 'I think I need to find Stan.'

'What has he done?'

'I... I'm not sure. You should leave now.'

He turned and looked out of the window. His gust of wind had blown out. And the fog was rolling back in from the sea.

Alice licked her lips and nodded. 'Will I get along the path?'

Dunkley turned back to her. 'I'll set it so you can.'

She hesitated on the threshold. 'Does it often happen? I mean do many of your people go bad?'

He looked at her in silence for a moment, then he said, 'I watch them all. I'm the strongest, as was Stan before me. That's how we keep ordinary people safe from us. As a whole the Church Officers watch Cræft users. But only one in each generation learns what can be done in the darkness. That was Stan, and that is now me. I think you should leave as quickly as possible.'

Under the shadow of his beard, his face looked like it was carved from white marble.

Alice collected her files from the wall as the fog dragged icy fingers over her neck.

Dunkley followed her out of the house. He retrieved his stick from beside the door and tapped three times on the gravel path.

'Hurry now,' he said.

Having been caught once in a supernatural fight, she needed no further urging. The sea fret curled back leaving the path clear to her car. Clutching the files to her chest, she trotted as fast as the tight skirt let her.

On either side of the path, muffled by the mist, she heard movement: scrabbling paws. She looked over her shoulder. Dunkley stood at his end of the clear road, holding his stick high. Behind him, the setting sun shone through the icy mist.

It split into three suns, joined together by an arc of light.

Alice increased her pace. Then Mr. Werlow stepped into the drive.

Dressed in his dark work suit, that looked so old-fashioned, he carried an incongruous bright red umbrella in his right hand, like a wand. Her umbrella that she had left at the house. He pointed it at her.

'I can't let you take those files, Alice,' he said.

Alice frowned. 'But they prove our client is innocent, Mr. Werlow.'

'Quite,' he said with a tight smile. 'But for what he did to her thirty years ago, he needs to be found guilty.'

'I beg your pardon?'

Alice glanced over her shoulder again. Why wasn't Dunkley rushing up to her rescue? He stood where she had last seen him—the fox stepped between them

She darted her glance back to Mr. Werlow.

Using the tip of the umbrella he drew a line across her path to the car. He laid the umbrella in the indentation of the gravel.

'Give me the files please, Alice.' He held out an imperious hand.

Alice clutched them tighter. 'Why don't you want our client to be free?'

'He drove his daughter to her death, him and the like-minded people of that village.' He smiled at Alice, but his eyes didn't see her. 'They're all dead now.'

Alice snapped her mouth shut over her next words. She grasped it was never a good idea to let a murderer know she recognized him.

Behind her Dunkley shouted. 'Alice could you tie your shoe when you get to your car.'

Alice gaped. She was wearing court shoes, without laces.

Mr. Werlow snapped out of his daydream. 'What's he doing here? He's early.'

Still holding the files in a white knuckled grasp, Alice tried to pass him. Her car waited 50 meters away. With her free hand, she fumbled for the keys in her pocket.

The line Mr. Werlow had drawn with her umbrella stopped her foot, not one toe could cross the line. He smiled his distant smile at her.

There was only one place of safety. Alice spun and charged the fox. It skipped out of the way, but snapped at her skirt hem.

She turned and batted at its snout with the legal files. From the corner of her eye she saw Mr. Werlow raise his arms.

'Mr. Dunkley!' she screamed. 'He's here.'

The mist rolled over her, muffling the shout. Misty tendrils reached into her nostrils, mouth, ears.

Squinting she could barely see the hand held out in case she ran into an unseen tree. The fox sang out its lonely call. She could feel the yapping spinning an illusion from her past.

The trumpet rang out again. People circled the fire holding lighted fire torches. Her stepbrother, Karl lay on the altar.

- No, I'm not here.

Her cousin Penny struggled as the ground turned to mud under her feet. They let Penny sink

- Penny is alive.

Lightning crackled in the air. Alice felt the power building.

'NO!' she screamed. 'I'm not here!'

In her head she built the image of the poplar-bordered drive, with safety in the form of Dunkley at the end.

She staggered. Her feet crunched on the gravel. She envisioned the heat from the fire torches driving away the mist.

Still clawing for her, it rolled back reluctantly.

'Alice,' Mr. Werlow's voice rasped her ears. 'Come here with those files.'

Refusing to look over her shoulder, she set her eyes on her goal of safety. Dunkley sprinted in slow motion towards her, his dogs bounding first.

He was coming. She just had to stay free of Mr. Werlow.

More mist dropped in front of her vision. This time it was solid. Cobwebs wrapped around her, strong as steel hawsers. They tangled her legs and she fell to the gravel.

With her arms tied to her body, she was unable to catch her fall. The sharp stones cut into her face and neck, and her legs below the skirt.

She felt as a ladder ran down her tights.

The fox snapped at her face.

She turned her nose into the gravel, but felt the fangs tearing at her ear. A hot trickle of blood ran down her neck.

She tried hunching into a ball, but the webs kept her flat and gagged her scream.

The gravel crunched as someone walked closer.

'Alice, that was silly,' Mr. Werlow said. 'Now I'm going to have to take the files the hard way. You shouldn't have come here. I loved having you as my assistant, you're so like her. I was going to ask you to marry me. He told me you were Alison re-incarnated. We'd have been happy here, together at last.'

Again the webs muffled her scream. She thrashed about trying to free some part of her body from the web.

'Now,' he continued. 'I'm going to have to wait until you come again. It's a long wait, sweet Alice, sweet Alison.'

The fox tore at the webs near her face and Alice realized that it was exposing her neck. She wriggled harder.

Then a low growl sounded.

For a moment Alice thought it was the fox, but the sound was deeper. Even through the masking web she saw one of those brute wolfhounds stalking the fox. The other tracked Mr. Werlow as he backed away from Alice.

'Stan? What are you doing, Stan?' Dunkley's voice sounded like a growl.

The ground felt like it was rolling under her. She could feel the forces building in the air, just like that night when her mother and uncle had summoned forces they couldn't control—and died—killing her father as well.

'They drove her to her death, but I loved Alison,' Werlow said. 'I had prepared this house. We could live as husband and wife.'

The ground swayed as the men played a spectral tug of war. Alice was grateful she was lying down.

'You know our vows,' Dunkley said.

'Only you could blame me for love,' Werlow said. 'How could you understand love, Alasdair? You've tied yourself away from human emotion since your mother's death. Between Alison and me flowed love so strong that the ghost of her unborn son returned to me as an animal.'

Alice could see the images the fox was building. The happy home, just kill this one, then he could be free to wait again. She managed to move her left hand and ripped at the encasing webs. They tickled and itched on her damp face.

'No one can return once they are dead.' Dunkley laid images of peace and calm.

Alice felt travel-sick, as her eyes told her the land was still but other senses said that everything was moving.

'*He* did!' Werlow shouted. 'The ghost of a murdered child can return as an animal to lead the way to his murderers.'

'You know that's nonsense,' Dunkley said, softly.

That's not the way to persuade him. Alice desperately tore at the web near her hand. She had to get her face free.

She dug her nails through the strands and felt damp, cold air on her fingertips.

'And that's Alison, returned again.'

'That way is madness, old friend,' said Dunkley. 'It doesn't happen like that. Come back. That is Alice Carsden, daughter of Gordon. You taught him.'

'My ghost son told me that this was his mother,' said Werlow.

'In the same way he told you to kill the people who killed his mother?'

'They needed to be punished,' said Werlow. 'By withholding the evidence that would free the old man, I will punish Alison's father. You should understand, you use your position to keep your father in that mental hospital.'

'Stan, I don't want to hurt you.'

'That's your weakness, boy. You always try and spare people.'

Lightning crackled from Werlow's hands.

Dunkley ducked to the side and behind a poplar.

Fire ripped up the tree trunk.

Dunkley backed to the next tree.

Alice tore at the cobwebs. Never mind bananas, these spiders must eat iron ore. She clawed at the web to free the other hand. Gasping for breath, she pulled the web from her face.

'This is the time of the Ghost Son,' Werlow shouted. 'You can see the ghost sun in the sky. There are two of them tonight. They give me the strength to defeat you.'

'That's a simple parhelion,' said Dunkley, dodging another fire-strike. 'Light reflecting through ice crystals in the mist. There's nothing mystical in it.'

'You've worked with mystics and magic all your life, and still you don't believe,' said Werlow. 'Didn't I teach you anything, boy? Belief strengthens all that we do.'

Finally she had her face free. Alice let her mind sink into the power they summoned. She could taste the energy as lightning crackled in the mist. Both men were wrapped in a black aura of doubt and despair. It felt like they were standing inside a thundercloud.

Dunkley dodged out from behind the tree and vaulted the low wall surrounding the cottage.

Werlow stamped his foot and power flowed. An earthquake rolled towards the cliff, sending Dunkley sprawling over the path to the front door.

A chuck of rock crumbled from the edge and crashed into the sea below. Werlow lifted his hands, calling the lightning.

'No!' Alice pulled at the itching strands that still draped her forehead.

Both men looked at her. The fox peered from behind Mr. Werlow's legs, where it hid from the wolfhounds. The power smell intensified.

'It's in the sunset,' she babbled. 'If it was sunrise, then I'd agree with you, Mr. Werlow, but a sunset is the ending of something.'

Werlow glanced at the sun, and back to Alice.

Believe it, she prayed. 'The Ghost sun is calling you both home.'

The fox curled back its lips in a snarl. It whispered its song of the laughing children and the singing wife rocking the cradle.

Pulling at the web of power summoned by both men, Alice wove the image the fox gave him into the three suns on the horizon.

'Hurry,' she said. 'The sun is setting. This is the last chance for you and your ghost son to find Alison.'

Werlow turned to the sunset. He grabbed the fox by its scruff.

Lifting it off its feet he ran into the setting sun. He smiled.

'Wait for me, Alison!' he shouted as he ran off the cliff edge.

There was no scream.

With tears adding to the damp on her face Alice whispered, 'Adieu.'

Dunkley scrambled to his feet, his eyes as black and cold as night. 'I wasn't going to kill him!'

'What were you going to do?' demanded Alice, peeling layers of web from her once-best linen suit. 'Bung him up in the mental home next to your dad?'

'Laird Dunkley killed his wife,' shouted Dunkley. 'In front of their nine-year-old son. For the crime of refusing to bear any more children to such a violent man and taking a contraceptive pill. A privilege you will take as a right. Don't you think he deserves to rot in hell?'

'Yes I do.' Alice glanced up at him. The blackness in his eyes sucked in the remains of the sunlight. 'But could you have locked up Mr. Werlow too?'

Panting hard, Dunkley spun and raised his hands over his head.

Alice watched him from where she huddled on the ground and saw blue lightning crackle from his fingers. It arched between his hands. His body exuded a blue glow, almost hiding his dark aura.

'Burn!' he shouted.

From the ground around the house, flames erupted, engulfing the building in seconds. Alice clutched the notes to her chest as the inferno scalded her cheeks.

'Burn!' His voice cracked as he shouted a second time.

As Alice watched, Dunkley buckled at the knees.

He sank to the ground, rocking on his knees, hands pressed to his eyes. His back trembled under wracking sobs.

Too shaky to stand herself, Alice got to her hands and knees and crawled over to him.

'Mr. Dunkley?'

He took no notice as he knelt, rocking.

'Alasdair,' she said. 'The man he once was would have wanted you to do this.'

He nodded, still with his hands pressed to his face. 'He taught me for this eventuality—as I will have to teach someone.'

Alice touched his shoulder. 'He was your mentor.'

'He was more than that,' whispered Dunkley, hoarsely. 'After Laird Dunkley killed my mother, Stan was...'

'He was like a father to you.'

Dunkley nodded again. Alice turned away to give him the privacy to regain his composure. As she watched the house collapse with the intensity of the fire, the sun pulled the two ghost suns with it, below the horizon.

Tricks of the Trade

'You don't know what I'm talking about do you? Let me show you,' said Ryan Kicksie. He pulled out a small penknife.

The woman at the door smiled her encouragement. Brushing back a wisp of her gray hair, she said, 'Yes show me these beadings.'

Josh stood back, grinning as he watched Ryan work his magic: to convince someone who already has double-glazing to buy a new set. Off on the Village Green he saw two dogs competing for the pleasure of returning a ball to their master. When they raced back to their owner, Josh could see they were huge, reaching his waist. He dragged his mind back to Ryan's droning voice. Through the open door Josh could smell newly baked biscuits.

'As you can see, madam, this beading comes out quite easily and a burglar could get into your house. All the insurance companies are going to insist on the new style of windows shortly,' said Ryan with a sad smile. 'Or else use the lack of them to hike up your insurance premiums.'

'Oh that's dreadful,' said the woman. 'Why don't you two boys look around my house and give me an estimate for how much it would be to replace the windows? Only the downstairs ones you understand. I couldn't afford a full refit. Walk around the house, but please keep to the path, and we can discuss the price over tea on the back patio.'

The woman closed the door.

'And there you have it, Josh,' said Ryan, leading the way around the back of the house. 'Count the windows as we go past. You have to convince them of a new threat. Then they'll want your product.'

'There's one window on the front, and the main door,' said Josh.

'Now you've got this wrong, kiddo,' said Ryan. 'It's your first day, so learn quick. You've got to give them the price for a full refit first, horrify them at the huge cost, then you can give them the lower price for the partial refit. The old lady'll jump at it.'

Josh followed, while counting windows. He felt his conscience prick, as he thought of the lady, who reminded him of his granny. It was the little things, everything was spotless, but there were signs, the threadbare mat on the front doorstep and the rusting black paint on the gate into the back garden, that said there was very little money here, and now Ryan had frightened the woman. If she lived alone she'd be very scared of burglars—his granny was.

The woman waited for them on her back patio. Ryan halted and counted the windows here at the back. Then he pulled out a notebook and started doing calculations.

Josh looked around. The path wove through the untrimmed lawn rather than going straight to the back door; dandelion heads told the time in the light summer breeze—wildflower meadow, that's what the gardening shows called grass like this. A dragonfly darted over a natural pond. It settled for a moment on a lily pad, then a frog crunched it.

There were no weeds in the tended flowerbeds, but they did have stones that looked too heavy to move. Was that really a stone? It had writing on it. He peered down. It was a book, what an odd garden ornament.

No! He could see the rotting pages. He bent over to get a closer look. The gold leaf had flaked away but it clearly said *Holy Bible*. He stepped back, hand out to grab Ryan's arm. His hand touched nothing. Panic! Where was Ryan?

For a moment he thought that the man had vanished, but he had only walked away up the path.

'Come on, Josh,' said Ryan. 'Nice garden you've got here, madam. I like your pond. Cast your eyes on this fish. It's green. Is that a Koi Carp? I hear they are difficult to keep.'

'Not this one,' said the woman. 'I'm glad to hear that you like my pond.'

Ryan muttered to Josh, 'She's got ghoulish taste in pond ornaments. Down there, see, her fish has a skull to swim in and out of.'

Josh noticed that he had back-pedaled from the pond when he banged against the garden gate. He looked over at the woman on the patio. She had a fixed smile on her face. It didn't touch her eyes. Somehow she seemed younger than his granny now.

She lifted her arms. The green fish popped its face out of the water.

'Oooo! Ith thith a new toy for Jenny?' lisped the fish.

What? Josh's mouth dropped open. Fish don't talk. He glanced at the woman, expecting to see a remote control. She had her arms folded across her chest, a satisfied smirk on her face.

Josh heard splashing.

It looked like a pond fountain was blowing water up from the surface of the pond, just where the fish had been. It swirled in a vortex pattern and coalesced into the form of a greenish-faced woman. With duckweed-draped arms, she reached for Ryan—who stood there gawking. His mouth hung open and his eyes boggled as he looked at the impossible woman.

'Come to Jenny Greenteeth, toyboy.' Her smiling lips opened to reveal a shark's maw.

Josh's hand fumbled at the gate latch. It stuck fast under his groping fingers. 'Ryan!' he screamed.

The cry snapped the hypnosis. Ryan backed up. He stepped off the path and onto the ill-tended lawn. On the patio the woman giggled.

'There's your playtoy, Jenny.'

'He'th getting away,' shrieked Jenny.

Josh noticed that fish woman moved sluggishly on land. Her long gown of duckweed had a train that led back into the pond water. The sleeves of her gown writhed with a life of their own. Josh could see why Ryan dared not turn away from Jenny, even with her slow pace. Like tentacles, the long fronds reached out to coil around Ryan's foot. Frantically, he tugged and kicked, but the duckweed held. He bent down and shoved the tendrils over his foot, but lost a shoe. He continued backing up towards the gate, kicking at the fronds as they got near.

The old woman made a flicking motion with her hand.

Ryan's foot caught in a rusty rake that lay in the grass. Josh had seen that happen in cartoons, but he never thought it could happen in real life. The pole slammed up and thwacked Ryan in the back of the head. He buckled at the knees. A frond of duckweed wrapped around Ryan's waist and hauled him towards the water.

Still dazed by the rake, he weakly pushed at the wrapped weed. With fingers that didn't want to work he ripped and tore until strands of duckweed tied his fingers together.

Josh stood at the gate, staring at the impossible thing that was happening before him.

'Josh!' Ryan screamed. 'Help me!'

Josh took half a step forwards, trying to think what he could do.

Seeing a rescue attempt, Jenny grinned and hauled on the duckweed strand.

'Help!' Ryan screamed again.

The duckweed crept up his body as it dragged him over the gravel path. It grew over his mouth and muffled his terror.

His feet touched the pond. He bucked and squirmed, like a walrus on land, trying to get away from the water.

Josh took another step. Then he darted forwards and grabbed a stone from the flowerbed and chucked it at Jenny. It missed and splashed in the water behind her.

Laughing, Jenny bent down and wrapped her arms around Ryan and kissed him. She melted into the water, dragging Ryan down with her. The water sprayed at his frantic struggles, then it went calm.

Josh swallowed.

'Jenny, there's another toy for you.' The old woman tutted at having to remind Jenny Greenteeth.

The frog-like face condensed from the water again, like rain falling upwards. Her eager eyes remembered Josh. Another frond sped for him. He turned to try and wrench open the gate, but it was jammed. He rattled it and tried to climb, but with those spikes on top he had no chance of getting over.

'Oh God!' he shouted.

Dancing around the sucking fronds, he grabbed the rake that had felled his partner and clawed at the reaching monstrosity. The rake snapped the fronds. From the broken woody stem, ichor oozed and where it dripped the grass turned black. The tentacle-like frond curled back, but Jenny reached out her other arm and her sleeve was already sliding through the long grass.

Josh prepared his rake again, eyes white in horror and disbelief. This didn't happen. On the patio the woman threw back her head and cackled.

'You and that fool thought you could take advantage of an ignorant old woman,' she shouted. 'I went to University when it was an honor to get accepted. I took physics when it "wasn't a subject for girls." I have ten times your pitiful intelligence and you patronized me.'

'I'm sorry,' shouted Josh as he wielded the rake. 'I'm really sorry.'

'Not sorry enough,' said the woman. 'Not yet.'

Through the tears that dripped down his cheeks, Josh saw Jenny walk slowly towards him, the hem of her dress still dragging in the water. He pulled his rake through the next sleeve-frond, ripping away more duckweed. He backed down the path hitting out at the reaching limb. Could he get past Jenny and cut her link to the water? Perhaps that would stop the creature.

It was the only chance he had. The fronds from the duckweed curled around his ankle. He could feel the slime on the leaves as they touched skin under his trousers.

'Come to Jenny, little toy.'

Unable to control his racing breath, his knuckles turned white as he gripped the rake in both hands. Only one chance. Only one chance. The mantra ran round his head. The fronds of duckweed tugged him and he walked forwards.

'What a good little toy,' said Jenny. She smiled, baring her green fangs.

Only one chance.

Josh dived behind Jenny and pulled his rake across the connecting train of duckweed. He had to break the link to water.

Jenny screamed as the fronds split and leaked their ichor over gravel and grass.

'Mithtreth. He'th hurting me.'

The woman on the patio raced to the steps. Lying across the path, with duckweed tightening around him, Josh lifted the rake again. He flung it across the weed and tugged back.

Jenny Greenteeth screamed again. She turned. Her puzzled little child's face had turned into a gaping maw. The teeth bore down on Josh.

With a great clang the garden gate burst open. Two huge dogs bounded over him as if in some grim competition to reach the monster first.

'Ross, Rory, *Murt*,' shouted a man running around the side of the house. The dogs immediately attacked the green woman. She tried retreating into the pond, as the dogs savaged her with their gleaming fangs.

The man planted a staff into the gravel path and shouted, '*The ungodly have laid a snare for my unwary feet.*'

Something spread out from him—Josh could feel it in the shiver that went down his spine, as if the light of the sun had momentarily dimmed.

The fronds of duckweed tore from around his body and followed Jenny Greenteeth as she melted back into the pond. Soaking and covered in flecks of green slime, Josh pushed to his feet, using the garden rake.

The woman on the patio bowed her head. She had sagged back into being an old woman.

'I can't let you do this any more, you know.' The man had a faint Scottish accent.

She looked up, a wistful smile on her face. 'Not even the irritating missionaries?'

Josh's eyes flicked to the rotting Bible in the flowerbed.

'Lead me not into temptation,' said the man, but his brown eyes held a hint of laughter in them.

'Come and talk with me,' said the woman. 'Take tea, I've got fresh baked cookies. At my age, trashing the patronizing cold callers is one of the few pleasures left, you know.'

The man strode past Josh and his rake, and up the three steps onto the patio. Looking around for more danger, Josh saw that the dogs had driven the last fronds back into the pond. The dogs growled at the thrashing water. He looked back to watch the confrontation.

The man stepped suddenly on the woman's shadow. 'I bind your hospitality by your shadow.'

She whispered something. Again, Josh felt a shivery something, but this time it fizzled out like a damp firework. She flung her head back and glared at the man.

'That's not fair, using one of our tricks,' the woman hissed. 'I'm bound to you, witch finder. And you've put a null on my garden.'

Then the man glanced over his shoulder. 'I don't think highly of your self-preservation instinct,' he said to Josh. 'Now would be a good time to run, while I'm distracting her.'

Josh looked at the man, the rake, and the pond. The dogs guarded the edge of the water growling and snapping as the water roiled like a Jacuzzi.

'She summoned a...a... a bloody kraken to her garden pond,' shouted Josh. 'It ate Ryan.'

He dropped the rake and scarpered. The house was down a lane outside of the village. Every hedge and ditch seemed to hide something that had once lurked under his bed as a child. His mother had convinced him that monsters were afraid of water. She had taken a spray bottle of water around his room and squirted the dark corners where the monster hid—after all monsters were allergic to water. But now he knew how wrong she had been.

Then he was in the center of the village. He slammed down onto a seat, looking at the duck pond. That creature had lived in the garden pond. He scrambled away, backing into a man, who grabbed at him so as not to fall over.

'What your problem, son?'

'That old woman! She killed him!'

The man backed away from him. 'Are you all right boy? Been taking those drugs instead of lunch have you?'

'No!' said Josh. 'The police. That's it, I need the police.'

He yanked the company mobile phone out of his pocket as the man fled. Josh retreated from the village duck pond and punched in the emergency number. Once through to the police he gabbled, 'She killed him. My partner, she killed him. I nearly didn't get away but the other man came.'

The operator calmed him down and got the information from him. Within minutes two cars with flashing blue lights pulled into the village and picked him up. They'd got the important part, that someone was dead.

Josh directed them up the lane. The company van parked where Ryan had left it, in front of the old house.

The front door opened and the old woman came out.

Before Josh could speak she shouted, 'That's one of them, officer. Don't let him get away. There were two of them. Drunk, cavorting about my back garden, threatening me. One of them fell in the garden pond then this one ran away. I didn't know what to do. I don't have a phone, thank goodness you've turned up.'

The senior officer went to speak to her. After listening to her story, he gestured and two more went with the senior officer around to the back of the house. The remaining officer kept an eye on Josh.

Josh got out of the police car and leaned up against the company van. The keys were at the bottom of the pond, with Ryan, or he'd have driven away.

The senior officer returned looking grave. 'I'm afraid the account by the householder does not tally with your story of giant walking pond plants. But we have found the body of a man. We need you to come and identify him for us.'

Josh licked his lips, but let the policeman lead him around the house.

The rake lay across the path just as he had dropped it when he fled. There was a body, half in half out of the water. A green fish sniffed around the floating hair. Two policemen were dragging Ryan's head out of the water.

'Now he appears to have a bang on the back of his head,' said the officer. 'Can you explain how that happened?'

'He was backing away from...' He stopped. Now his first panic-ridden flight was over he began to see just how insane his story was. He was in big trouble.

But he knew what had happened. From the window he could see the woman looking out at him. There were daggers in her eyes when she saw him, but the old lady's simper returned as one of the policemen turned her way.

'That rake hit him when he stepped backward off the path.'

One of the policemen picked up the rake in gloved hands. It was bagged.

'I'm going to have to ask you to accompany me to the station, sir,' said the senior. 'I will have someone come and tow the vehicle away. Your company will be informed when it can be retrieved.'

Josh sagged. He had no idea how to explain this away. And his fingerprints would be all over that rake. From what he could see there was no evidence to support being attacked by a monstrous creature. He closed his mouth and kept it that way as he was taken to the police car.

Across the road a man watched proceedings. Josh looked at him incuriously, then he realized it was the man who had come running. Sitting at his feet were those two huge dogs that had driven the monster away.

'He can tell you what happened,' shouted Josh, pointing at the man.

The policemen looked over the road. They squinted and looked away. Josh could see the man looked surprised.

'Where?' said the officer. 'Is this just more of your stories?'

'No he's there,' he said pointing.

The man stepped over the road.

'Oh,' said the officer. 'Didn't see you in that shadow, sir. This boy seems to think that you know something about what happened here today.'

Josh could see why the policeman was respectful, those dogs looked menacing. Their heads were level with the man's hips. The man ignored the policeman.

'You don't look old enough to be working, what's your age, boy?'

Josh suddenly felt everything would be taken care of. 'I'm eighteen. My mum said that since I'd done so poorly on my A levels I would have to take a job as no university would take me. So I applied for this. This is my first day on the job.'

'And the last one?'

'Oh yes!' Josh said. 'I'm finding something else.'

The man nodded. He turned to the police officer and produced his wallet. 'I think I can explain what has gone on today.'

He flipped out a business card and held it out to the senior officer, so that no one else could see it. The officer palmed it. Checking it, he looked up with a mixture of horror and awe on his face.

The man asked, 'What did the woman of the house say happened here?'

The officer cleared his throat. 'She says those two young men, danced about her lawn shouting threats and bad words. She took them to be drunk, then one of them stepped on the rake, and fell in the pond. The other young man, this one, ran away.'

'I think that is what happened here too,' the man said. He turned to go. 'Come with me, Joshua.'

'It's all right sir. I'm sure he won't tell anymore tall stories about your dogs attacking walking plants.' The policeman put a hand on Josh's arm and squeezed a warning. 'I can escort the young man home to his mum.'

'I will deal with him now.'

How did he know my name? Josh thought.

Reluctantly, the senior police officer let go of Josh's arm.

Josh stepped over to the man and fell in beside him as he walked down the lane. Parked to one side was a people carrier. The man opened this up and fastened his dogs into safety harnesses in the rear.

Josh got in the passenger seat. 'Why was the policeman afraid of you? Why didn't he want me to go off with you?'

The man started the car. 'He thinks I'm going to kill you.'

Josh looked startled. 'What?'

'They only ever find those cards on bodies that have died in, shall we call them, *unusual* circumstances.'

'Are you going to kill me?

'Not today.'

'Who are you?'

'I'm Dunkley. I work for the Church. It would be easiest if you think of me as a witch finder.' Dunkley looked at Josh then set his car in motion.

'You shouldn't have been able to see me. Would you like a job?'

'I'd get to learn that magic, like you did?'

Dunkley winced. 'I don't do magic, Joshua. I utilize Practical Theology. There is a big difference.'

'But I'd be fighting things like that?' asked Josh.

'On a regular basis.'

Josh looked at his hands. They were covered in mud and scratches. He looked up. 'When do I start?'